MW00905201

PICTURE ME

LORI WEBER

JAMES LORIMER & COMPANY LTD., PUBLISHERS
TORONTO

Copyright © 2013 by Lori Weber
First published in the United States in 2014.

All rights reserved. No part of this book may be reproduced or transmitted in any form or by any means, electronic or mechanical, including photocopying, or by any information storage or retrieval system, without permission in writing from the publisher.

James Lorimer & Company Ltd., Publishers acknowledges the support of the Ontario Arts Council. We acknowledge the financial support of the Government of Canada through the Canada Book Fund for our publishing activities. We acknowledge the support of the Canada Council for the Arts which last year invested $24.3 million in writing and publishing throughout Canada. We acknowledge the Government of Ontario through the Ontario Media Development Corporation's Ontario Book Initiative.

  Canadä

Cover design: Meghan Collins
Cover image: istockphotography

Library and Archives Canada Cataloguing in Publication

Weber, Lori, 1959-, author
    Picture me / Lori Weber.

Issued in print and electronic formats.
ISBN 978-1-4594-0509-7 (bound).--ISBN 978-1-4594-0510-3 (pbk.).--
ISBN 978-1-4594-0511-0 (epub)

    I. Title.

PS8645.E24P52 2013   jC813'.6   C2013-904173-7
C2013-904174-5

James Lorimer & Company Ltd.,   Distributed in the United States by:
Publishers   Orca Book Publishers
317 Adelaide Street West, Suite 1002   P.O. Box 468
Toronto, ON, Canada   Custer, WA, USA
M5V 1P9   98240-0468
www.lorimer.ca

Printed and bound in Canada.
Manufactured by Friesens Corporation in Altona, Manitoba, Canada in August 2013.
#87633

*To girls everywhere who just want to be themselves,
without fear.*

ÉCOLE CHAMPS VALLÉE SCHOOL

CHAPTER ONE

Krista rises slowly out of her chair. I keep my eyes on her face so that if she looks over she'll know I'm with her. If I could, I'd stand up too and read the poem out loud, but Ms. Bane didn't call on me. I had to read the first stanza of "Barbie Doll," the one about how the girl played with *GE stoves and irons* and *wee lipsticks* when she was a kid, back when she was happy. Before she grew up and someone crushed her by telling her that she had a *great big nose and fat legs.*

Krista clears her throat. Giggles are already rising from the back of the class like bubbles. Krista shrugs her shoulders and begins.

In the casket displayed on satin she lay
with the undertaker's cosmetics painted on,
a turned-up putty nose,
dressed in a pink and white nightie.

A medley of woo-woos floats up, like a prearranged chorus. Krista's cheeks turn red under her dark hair. I pray that Ms. Bane will let her sit down now, but she doesn't. She nods for Krista to continue.

Doesn't she look pretty? everyone said.
Consummation at last.
To every woman a happy ending.

Krista's voice goes soft on the last two words, as if she wants to bury them. She slides into her chair just as Chelsea calls out, "Better late than never." Ms. Bane lets out a big sigh but doesn't say anything.

It's pretty obvious Chelsea didn't get the point of the poem. Here was a smart, normal girl, just going along minding her own business, until people started making her think she was fat and ugly. Okay, it's not really possible to cut off your nose and legs like the girl in the poem did, but that's why it's poetry, not real life. It's a metaphor. I don't understand why Ms. Bane isn't pointing that out.

"Two hundred words on a possible theme of Marge Piercy's poem, for tomorrow," says Ms. Bane.

A collective groan ascends. I hear Chelsea's groan above all the others.

I can imagine what she'll write — that the girl finally smartened up by turning herself from fat but happy into a skinny mess. The inside of Chelsea's locker is plastered with pictures of movie stars. In computer class, when we're supposed to be looking up topics like the history of the cotton trade in America or the Battle of Little Bighorn, Chelsea looks up celebrity photos on TMZ. I peeked over her shoulder once and saw Paris Hilton standing outside her house. It was so big, it looked like six houses stuck together under the same red-tiled roof. There were security cameras all around the perimeter to keep out the riff-raff. I guess the shot was taken by some paparazzo hanging out of a helicopter, risking his life for that one, perfect, big-pay shot.

On the way out of class, Chelsea pushes right up against Krista and says, "Hey, gonna cut off your nose and legs and offer them up? Don't waste your time. No one would want them."

Her look-alike friend, Amber, chimes in. "Yeah, not even a carnivorous monster who hasn't eaten in a hundred years."

"But if you do kill yourself and get a new nose and loads of make-up, maybe we could finally stand to look at you," Chelsea adds.

Then they flip their Hollywood hair and saunter off, cracking up.

I am beside Krista but I don't know what to say. I never do. Over the years, we've both fallen into the pattern of ignoring girls like Chelsea and Amber. Today is no different. Krista looks straight ahead, eyes on the chemistry lab where her next class is. If nasty things happen to her there, I don't know about them. Chances are it's not so bad because Chelsea is in computers, with me.

Sometimes I think I can feel Krista's relief when we say goodbye and she watches Chelsea walk away.

Sometimes, I strip down to my undies and look at myself in the full-length mirror that is glued to the back of my door. I start with my feet. They're actually small, smaller than you'd think. They don't look like feet that were made to support someone who is five foot four and weighs one hundred and eighty pounds. They look like feet that were meant to support someone dainty, like one of those porcelain Chinese dolls. I stare at my feet for a long time because they're my favourite feature. After that, it's disappointment, all the way up.

My calves and thighs are really round. My mom says I have those three diamond-shaped spaces between my legs that Marilyn Monroe was famous for: one above her ankles, another at her knees and one between her thighs. But I don't see the diamonds. I see one large blob of leg, thick like a tree trunk. I come way in at the waist, in proportion to my size, but under that waist is a big round belly and above it is a wide chest with big boobs. I know big boobs should be a good thing, but that's only on really skinny bodies, where the boobs stand out, like on models. On me, they don't. On me, they blend in with the sea of body surrounding them and just make me look bigger.

My mom says that if Marilyn Monroe were alive today she'd be considered heavy and would never even land a role in a movie. She says it to make me feel better, but it doesn't, because this is now, not sixty years ago when Marilyn Monroe was a star. And anyway, if Marilyn was so perfect, why did she die of a drug overdose?

The only part of my body that I like is my brain. It's a pretty good brain, like the girl's in the poem that Ms. Bane made us read today. At least it gets me really good marks. My teachers have all said I'm one of the best writers they've ever met. I've won our school's story competition for the last two years, even though no one knows but the teachers because I signed my name *Anonymous*. The only writing I put my name on is this journal, but that's because no one will ever see it.

I know there is so much more to life than the way a person looks. A whole part of my brain knows that and really believes it. So, the thing I can never understand is how I can know it but still envy skinny girls like Chelsea and Amber at the same time? It doesn't make sense. Maybe I'm what psychiatrists call schizophrenic: *schizo* meaning split and *phrenic* meaning brain — a perfect description of how I feel whenever I see one of those skinny girls that try so hard to be devastating. The voice in my head, the strong voice that likes to write and think about things, says *Oh my god, she is so pathetic*, but another voice says, *I wish I could be her*. I don't get it, having those two thoughts at once. It's like my feet and body — they don't go together.

CHELSEA

If I lived in Hollywood, the stars and I would be friends. We'd go shopping together in Beverly Hills, with our little dogs tucked into fancy purses. We'd wander in and out of all those chic boutiques, the kind that don't seem to sell much stuff.

I've always wondered why discount stores have loads of stuff in them, like piles and piles of cheap underwear with ugly pink and orange flowers. Or stacks of T-shirts in thin and scratchy material, three for ten. Or mountains of jeans with ugly yellow stitching. Stores like that always smell musty, like the clothes have already been worn. But expensive stores, like the ones I see pictures of in magazines, are practically empty. One whole glass shelf might hold three tops. Bars hanging by chains from the ceiling hold five shirts on hangers, with tons of space between them. And the back wall might display two pairs of high-heeled shoes, sitting there like works of art.

I think it's because the stuff in those stores is exclusive. I love that word: exclusive, as in the only one. It's something I dream about. Like, imagine being the only one in the world to have something, something everyone else notices and wants and envies you for. Other girls might try to be like you, but they couldn't be you. You'd be the original and everyone else would just be a cheap knock-off. Like Amber is to me.

My English teacher would faint if she heard me use the word exclusive. She thinks I don't have any vocabulary, or that I don't know how to read, or at least she must because she didn't call on me today to read that stupid poem. She never calls on me, which just proves that she thinks I'm dumb. I'm not going to bother writing that dumb assignment. I'll just write what I think the theme is here, in my diary, where Ms. Bane will never see it. It's that there are natural-born winners and losers. I am a winner. I don't need to kill myself to get attention. But girls like Krista and her pathetic friend Tessa are losers. Teachers call on them all the time, like they're the only ones who know things. But they're not. I know things too, just not the kind of things teachers care about.

CHAPTER TWO

After school, I pick up my sister Annie at her elementary school and head straight home. I keep my eyes down when we enter the courtyard and don't look around to see who's there. There's an old stone fountain in the middle, with a spout in the shape of a tulip. Water used to come spurting out but now the spout is just a huge ashtray, brimming to the top with cigarette butts and the skinny tips of joints. Amber is often down there, with or without Chelsea, because she lives in one of the three apartment buildings that surround the courtyard. Luckily, not the same one as me.

Making eye contact with Chelsea or Amber today would be fatal.

I live in a six-storey apartment building with ten units on each floor. The hallways haven't been washed or painted in ages and the lights are always burnt out. The floors are covered in grey tiles that are always coming unstuck. Three weeks ago my mom's shoe caught the corner of one, which sent her and our groceries flying. The mayonnaise and pickle jars smashed and broke, but the worst thing that broke was my mom's ankle. Now she's on crutches and can't go to her job at the Bean Sprout Café downtown.

Today, for some reason, I can't help thinking about that mansion I saw over Chelsea's shoulder, the one Paris Hilton lives in. I wonder what she would do if she had to live here. Would she find it as oppressive as I sometimes do? Everywhere I look says "run down and shabby" and that makes it hard to dream of nice things, things I might like to have one day. Or things I might like to get for my little sister Annie, who is only seven.

We haven't been home an hour when Annie comes running out of our room and down the hallway into the living room, where I am trying to do my homework.

"Do you like it?" she asks, her voice breathless. She holds out a piece of paper and I take it from her. I know what it will be. Annie's pictures are all the same: country scenes, with lakes and mountains, sometimes animals and birds, and always a big, round, yellow sun in the corner, sometimes with streaky clouds across it.

"It's really pretty, Annie," I say, smiling. I'm not lying. She is good. I just find it funny because she's never been to a place that looks like that. "Why don't you hang it up?"

Annie beams and grabs the tape off the coffee table. I watch her reach up on tippytoes to add her latest creation to the Annie Gallery, which is what we call the hall wall. Her long braid swings across her back like a pendulum.

"Tessa, time to start with supper," my mom calls from the kitchen.

"Coming," I say, closing my books. My homework will have to wait until later tonight, after I've helped with dinner and done the dishes.

Sometimes, I wish things were different. Like, if my father were still here, he could help out too. But he isn't here. Five years ago he was killed by a roadside bomb in Afghanistan. It was an IED, which is something I'd never heard of before. It stands for "improvised explosive device." We do improv at school, with Ms. Bane. It's where people shout out words like dog, taxi and skipping and you have to turn them into a real story, on the spot. An IED takes a lot more planning because it involves wires and chemicals and whatever else goes into a bomb, so I'm not sure why it's called improvised. But that's what the army says killed my dad.

Apparently, IEDs are almost always fatal if the vehicle you're in drives over one of them. There were eight soldiers in the truck. Five of them were killed instantly, two died later (one of those was my dad), and one survived. That's just about as fatal as you can get. Lots of Afghan people were killed too, coming home from the market. Sometimes I think about how, somewhere in Afghanistan, there might be a girl my age whose father was also killed in that attack and how maybe she and I have tons in common and don't even know it. Like, maybe she sometimes closes her eyes and tries to remember her father and what he looked like and sounded like, or even smelled like.

My strongest memory of him was the time he came home on leave when Annie was a baby. He fell to his knees, opened his arms, and scooped me up. The crook of his neck smelled like airplane fuel and sweat. When my mom put Annie in his arms he cried as hard as if he had just chopped a dozen onions.

My mom is chopping onions now, balanced on one crutch. She's a pro. At work I've seen her chop three dozen in ten minutes, piling them at the end of the cutting board like an icy mountain. She makes salads and soups with exotic names, like Tuscan Tomato Salad, Asian Asparagus Salad, Potage St-Jacques de Mont, and Bulgarian Butternut Soup. The owners, Karen and Matt, find the recipes and pass them on to her, but she barely needs to follow them, she's that good at cooking. She normally starts at six and ends at three, so she can be here for us when we get home from school around four.

"Whatever else you may be missing, you're always greeted by a loving face instead of an empty apartment. Remember that," my mom has said more than once.

By "whatever else" I know she means my father.

KRISTA

I can hear my mom bustling around, getting ready to leave for her shift at the neonatal ward in the hospital downtown. It's the same routine four days a week, Tuesday to Friday. Out the door at five in the afternoon and home at six in the morning, when my dad and I are still sleeping. Any minute now, after she's gone, my dad will knock on my door and ask what I want for dinner. I use the word *dinner* kind of loosely. When books talk about dinner they usually mean a sit-down affair, with plates and cutlery and a big table full of people reaching across to grab heaping bowls of home-cooked dishes. Dinner here for the past decade has been more a matter of *Who ya gonna call?* Will it be pizza or fried chicken, Mexican or Chinese? Our stack of delivery fliers reaches from the countertop to the ceiling. When I was younger my dad and I would play a game where we'd close our eyes and pull out two. Then, he'd hold them behind his back and I'd get to pick a hand. Sometimes, we'd add to the game by guessing when the food would arrive. Whoever came closest without going over didn't have to do the clean-up — throwing away the wrappers and napkins and sometimes washing a dish or two. If anyone looked in the window, they'd know my dad and I are related. They'd see us sitting side by side on the couch, sinking into the cushions, biting battered chicken or nabbing fries and dipping them in gravy.

Sometimes when we're eating I think about what my mom might be doing at the hospital. She helps prepare the bottles for babies whose mothers refuse to breastfeed. This makes her angry because she knows they're just thinking of themselves and that old-wives' tale about how breastfeeding will make their boobs droop. (As for me, I was breast fed until the age of three. I wonder if there was something in that breast milk that programmed me to be big — like super calories or something.) For the ones who do breastfeed, she teaches them how to hold the baby right and relax to get the milk to come on down. That's what it's called, like the milk is a contestant on *The Price is Right.*

Sometimes, my mom helps with the preemies. I can always tell when she's done this because she comes home with a glow about her, like she's just seen an angel. She explains it as being so close to death — the frail, puppy-like bodies of these two- and three-pound babies clinging to life. She says that dealing with the preemies, keeping their incubators clean or helping the moms and dads who sit at their sides stay comfortable, gives her a greater sense of purpose than anything else she has ever done.

She's always going on about feeding the babies, how important it is to get nutrients into those little bodies. I wonder what she thinks of the kind of nutrients my dad and I are putting into our bodies. I know my mom knows because we don't try to hide the boxes. It's like she chooses not to notice. Maybe because, if she really did, she'd have to do something to change it and she can't. She's too busy sleeping and showering and getting ready to go to work again. And she has to be on night shift — that's when they need her. She can't be in two places at once, can she?

CHELSEA

My mom's hoping I'll learn something in school that helps me get a job real fast so I can help her pay bills, but if I do get a job I'm going to use it to get far away from here. I want to live somewhere where people don't look tired all the time, like my mom does. My mom would need tons of plastic surgery to get back to how she used to look. She used to be pretty, before she had me and my two brothers who are older than me and live far away with their father. She said having and raising them for ten years made her lose her looks, especially because she was drinking a lot back then, all through her twenties. Then she left them and had me and I'm such a handful that I take even more of her pretty away, or at least she says I do.

I wish I had the type of mom who looks really good for her age, like Lindsay Lohan's. I've seen pictures of her and Lindsay together. They look like they're having fun, with shopping bags looped over their arms or posing at the end of a red carpet in matching gowns. The only time my mom and I go shopping together is when I need something, like a new pair of shoes for school — and then we fight over which ones to buy. She's always pulling me over to the cheap ones but they're

never the ones I want. She says as long as she's the one paying the bills I have to get what she says. When I'm old enough
to make my own money I can get what I want. I can't wait for
that to happen.

The other day I tried a self-tan lotion because I can't
afford to go to a tanning salon. I did it carefully, after a shower,
but I still made a huge mess and my mom yelled at me for
hours like her life was over because she'd have to buy a new
bath mat. She bought it at the dollar store so I didn't see the
big deal. I was doing her a favour by ruining it, it was so ugly.
Those big red flowers looked like road-kill, or like the plate of
tinned pasta and sauce that we usually end up eating for dinner. And she made me scrub the shower stall for an hour with
special powder. Sometimes, I think that if my mom could,
she'd buy a special brush and powder to scrub me out of her
life. If she hadn't had me she'd be free right now. My half-
brothers only get a card twice a year, on their birthdays and at
Christmas. They live with their dad and new mom and I can't
tell if she misses them or not because she keeps her voice
calm and looks down when she talks about them.

There's nothing about my mom's life that I admire, not
even her job. She works nine to five in an office downtown as
secretary to the vice-president of this company that makes
weird pieces of machinery. I've seen the catalogue. It's full of
bits and pieces of twisted steel, nothing important that anyone cares about. She says it's the best job she's ever had, and
she's had many. At Christmas her boss gives her a bottle of
perfume, the kind that has a cheap necklace wrapped around
the neck, and that seems to make her happy. It's going to take
so much more than that to make me happy.

CHAPTER THREE

I'm just about to write a math test when the school secretary knocks on the door and asks to see me.

"You've got to go pick your sister up at her school and take her home right away. We'll give you the money for a taxi," she says.

"Why do I have to go then?"

"Because she's too young to take a taxi alone." She makes a funny face and I know she's thinking about those perverted things you hear about that happen to little kids sometimes and doesn't want to say it.

I wave goodbye to Krista at the door. She's going to have to eat lunch alone, something both of us hate.

Annie's skin is green when I get there, the kind of green someone's skin might turn after too much partying or too many drugs. The media is always going on about drugs in schools. Once, TV cameras came to my middle school because kids were caught dealing in our schoolyard. People were scandalized because what was happening to today's youth and blah blah blah. But drugs have been around for a long time. I have a picture of my mom and dad when they met twenty years ago and it's not hard to imagine them getting high. They're both dressed all in black with dyed-black hair and piercings, and Dad is giving the finger to the camera.

When I asked my mom why my dad was such a rebel but joined the army, she said it was complicated. Then she went on about money and bills and education and all I could get from her answer was that my dad felt he had no choice. He twisted his f-you finger around a pen and enlisted eight years ago. He and I were at the mall in the afternoon when we saw four men in army uniforms sitting behind a long table. They were super friendly. One even tugged on my braids and called me cutie and before I knew it my dad was reading a pamphlet and scratching his chin. When we came home he told my mom he thought he had found a better job and a smile stretched across her face. Annie was in her belly, probably feeling my mom's joy right through her skin. When he told her the job was with the army, my mom's smile crashed and she had to sit down.

When we get home my mom takes one look at Annie and tells me I have to take her to the neighbourhood clinic. I take a good book along because I know we'll be there forever.

All around us kids are blowing their noses and coughing and hacking. I try to imagine what the air would look like if I had a super-powered microscope and could see the germs mingling together. We have pictures of germs in our science book and it's amazing how much they look like bugs. Some are round and red, others long and blue or fuzzy or striped. It's funny to think that our bodies are crawling with bacteria like that no matter how pretty we are on the surface.

The doctor doesn't look impressed that Annie is with her sister and not her mom. He shakes his head like he is about to say "typical" but I stop him real fast with my hardest look and say, "For your information, my mother cannot walk at the moment because she a broken ankle." But his look doesn't change. Now he's thinking that my dad probably knocks her around because that's what everyone thinks of the people who live where I live.

It turns out that Annie has the flu. She needs to stay home, drink fluids, and sleep. If she isn't better in a week, we have to bring her back. When he asks me if I think we can handle that I want to say, "No, could you please repeat those very complicated instructions because I am a little bit retarded, don't you know?" I want to be a doctor myself when I grow up but I will never treat people like they're stupid just because they're not wearing designer clothes.

On the way home, we see a group of people gathered on the sidewalk up ahead. I take Annie's hot hand and pull her back. Crowds never mean anything good and I don't want her to see whatever is in the middle of the circle. Suddenly, someone calls my name and I look up to see our neighbour. "It's your mother," she calls. "Come quick." I leave Annie and run. There is my mom on the ground, her crutches splayed out beside her.

"Mom, what happened?" I ask.

"Oh, Tessie, I wanted to come see how you got on. I thought I could make it."

It turns out my mom fell when her crutches got caught in a crack in the pavement and now she has twisted her one good ankle. It doesn't surprise me one bit that she tried to come meet us. The night before my big test to see if I could get into the enriched math and science at school, my mom read in a magazine that bananas are the magic test food. They calm you down and help you think straight. She went out right then to the nearest grocery store, a twenty-minute bus ride. She made me eat one at night and one again in the morning. It must've worked because I got in and I didn't think I could. Krista made it too, so I was really glad. We're both going to try to get into the enriched stream in high school too, next year.

But now, I might as well say goodbye to school for the next three weeks. I'll be too tired to study. My mom's on the sofa with a fresh cup of tea and an ice pack on her ankle, her casted foot beside it. Annie is in bed with a cool, damp towel on her forehead. She's already thrown up twice into the bowl I put beside her, and each time I dumped it into the toilet I felt bile rising in my throat.

Today has made me think about whether or not I still want to be a doctor. The idea came to me when my dad died. They tried to patch him up and save him in a hospital in Germany for a few days after the explosion. But it didn't work. I imagined that, if I'd been there, I would've worked faster. My hands would've flown over his open wound with the speed and skill of a concert pianist.

But right now, sitting exhausted on my bed, that desire is gone, flushed away down the toilet with Annie's sick.

My favourite teacher in elementary school had a snow globe collection lined up across the front of her desk. By mid-morning the globes would catch the sun and sparkle. Whole cities rose out of the water: Las Vegas, Paris and Rome. Or mythological creatures, like dragons and fairies. Every day, just before the final bell, our teacher would select one student to choose a globe and shake it. That student had to be someone who had done their homework, put up their hand to answer a question, and didn't talk while the teacher was talking. Someone like me. But I dreaded being chosen. Being chosen meant this:

Getting out of my chair and walking to the front knowing every pair of eyes was turning to follow me; standing at the front as everyone watched to see which globe I would pick; shaking it gently so that no part of my body, except my arm, jiggled; holding the globe in my palm as everyone watched the sparkly snow swirl around the skyscrapers of Manhattan, showering down over the Empire State Building where King Kong had rescued the pretty woman; counting down the seconds until the snow would settle and release me from being the centre of everyone's attention.

Navigating school is like being in a minefield. It's dodge this and dodge that and constantly try to hide and be invisible, especially on days when Tessa isn't at school. When I'm sixteen I might quit school and finish up at home. There's only one thing that scares me about this plan and it's the fact that I'll be able to eat more. I might turn into one of those super-big people they show on TV, the ones who have no life other than eating and getting bigger, marooned on their sofas.

So, why don't I do something about my weight? I think about it all the time, especially when I'm at home with my dad. I think about shaking up the routine, like you shake a snow globe. I could try cooking, but how? It's not like my mom is around to teach me and my dad obviously doesn't have a clue. On weekends my mom is tired from her job so we go out to eat or order in again, like during the week. The rest of the time we eat stuff that comes ready-made out of a box or can. The microwave is the most important appliance in our kitchen. In fact, we could get rid of the stove altogether and we wouldn't miss it, except for cooking frozen fries.

Sometimes, I dream of shopping. I go up and down the aisles at the grocery store, filling our cart with healthy stuff, like vegetables and chicken or fish. At home, I put the chicken in the oven to bake and steam the vegetables. Then I place the cooked chicken in the middle of our plates and ring it with broccoli and beans. I don't know what it tastes like, but I know that eating it will make my stomach shrink.

When I look down at my stomach, I imagine actual things in there, under my skin, like whole pieces of pizza, thick with pepperoni, taco shells full of ground beef, sauce and cheese, cans of Coke. It's like I never swallowed any of it, I just slipped it in through a slit.

I wonder if my dad ever dreams of good food. Does the way we eat even matter to him? When he's at work in his fork lift at the electronics warehouse, does he look down at himself as he pushes the pedals and think about his size? Does he think about how, one day, he might get so big he'll need to be lifted by one of the machines he loves to operate?

My dad says I have beautiful hair. It's dark brown and falls down my back in natural curls that he says remind him of Niagara Falls, where he and my mom had their honeymoon. Sometimes, when we're eating supper and watching TV, my dad will pick up one of my locks and let it fall over my shoulder and say, *You have princess hair, just like Rapunzel.* It makes me feel good inside when he says that, only then

I remember that he's my dad and it makes me feel weird because I wish it wasn't my dad saying something like that to me but somebody else, someone who doesn't have to love me just because they're related to me.

CHELSEA

Now everything will be different. Now that I've met Tyler.

I was hanging out at the park with Amber and he kept coming out of the pizzeria across the street with stacks of boxes and waving over at us. At first, we didn't wave back. He was way older than us, like in his twenties, but cute. After a while he came over and lit a joint. I love the way he did it so casually, like he was just lighting a cigarette. He didn't care who was around. When he passed it to me our eyes locked. It was like in the movies. I knew we'd click. He doesn't go to school. He blew me away when he told us he gave that up when he was fifteen. He didn't say it in a sorry way, like the dropouts they make us listen to in assemblies, the ones with the sad eyes.

He said I could ride with him, so I did. He blasted the music and I sang and he told me I could be a star, I have such a great voice. He touched my thigh when he said that but then pulled his hand back and said sorry. He's such a gentleman. My mother would never believe that, so I ducked when he made deliveries on my block.

Then he told me about his plan to open a chain of pizzerias called Tyler's Pizza Parlour. He said if we got along I could model for the poster. A fibreglass cut-out of me holding up a pizza would stand on top of all the delivery cars and an even bigger one in each pizzeria window. He has the uniform picked out already, a fire-engine-red waitress dress with a super-short skirt. He said I'd wear it with the top buttons open and my free hand held up with a hooked finger, as though I was luring everyone in. He said pizza sales would skyrocket with me up there.

My blood was so hot when he said that I needed to crack open the window.

Next time I ride with him, I'm going to let my skirt ride a bit higher. Maybe he'll put his hand on my thigh and leave it there. If he does, I'll part my legs a bit, like models do in pictures, just to let him know it's okay. After all, he just might be my fairy godfather.

CHAPTER FOUR

Two cartoon hearts are bouncing all over the screen and a voice-over is going on and on about health and nutrition, throwing out facts and figures about calories and blood pressure. One cartoon heart has a happy face, pumping blood around a normal-size body; the other one frowns as it pumps blood through an obese body. Then the normal one is lying on a beach chair, sipping a tall drink. But the obese heart is stooped over and sweating, showing how much harder it had to work.

Even though biology is a really important subject for me, I can't stop my mind from wandering. I babysat last night for Karen and Matt, the couple that owns the café where my mom works. I like going to their house. It's in a totally different part of the city, up on a hill. It's not fancy inside, though. In fact, it's usually a mess, but it's a mess of interesting things, like books and bright, woven blankets and pottery. There are stacks of food and cooking magazines everywhere, with holes where recipes have been cut out.

My favourite part is after I put the kids to bed, when I can pull books off their shelves. They have a whole bookcase full of big fat books with pictures in them that I love to look at, with titles like Trekking in the Andes, Kenyan Safari, Florentine Masterpieces, and Up the Nile in Style. Every time I'm there, it's like I'm travelling to an exciting part of the world. Karen and Matt often come home to find Kim and Ian in bed and me asleep on the sofa with an open book collapsed on my chest. They always encourage me to take the book home to finish looking at it, but I don't. I prefer to look when I'm at their place. It's easier to dream when you're somewhere else.

There's one book on their shelf I haven't looked at yet: Buddhas of Afghanistan. Every time I go to take it down something stops me. I know it will be full of pictures of the country where my father spent the last two years of his life. He said he had no choice, that he had to go where the army sent him, but he had a choice about going back the second time for another tour of duty. My mom says I shouldn't be angry, that he was just trying to make money to support us. But his duty included being there for me and Annie. If I look at the book, I know I will picture him down on his belly in the sand, aiming his rifle at the caves or sitting cross-legged in a rubble hut. Like in the pictures on TV.

My mom tries to turn the channel when news comes in from Afghanistan but it's not like we can pretend it away. My mom could've joined a support group to meet other people who lost someone in the war, but she wasn't interested. She never saw us as a military family. We never lived on a base or went to the barbeques and picnics, waving little flags. My mom said she couldn't do that. She'd always been against war, so to start mixing with people who were really into the military way of life would just be strange. She said we could cope on our own, in our own way, thank you very much.

We did get some money from the army for my dad's death. My mom spent days and days filling out forms. A whole pile of red tape, she called it. The money wouldn't seem like a huge sum to some people but to us it was a fortune. It took forever to get it, though. My mom says they dragged their heels, as if the money itself was buried deep in the caves of Afghanistan. She put most of it straight into a college fund for me and Annie, which is what she said my dad would have wanted her to do. In his letters home, he said one of the saddest things about Afghanistan was how the Taliban, the bad guys, had closed all the schools for girls and didn't even let them leave home unless they had a man or boy to escort them. I can't imagine what that would be like. What would me, my mom, and Annie have done in that situation, all these years?

Suddenly Krista is shaking my shoulder. "Wake up, Tessa," she says. "Show's over."

I must have day-dreamed right through the bell. Maybe my mom's right — I shouldn't babysit on a weeknight. But I'm saving up for a computer for high school.

We're halfway up the stairwell on our way to the cafeteria when Chelsea and Amber block our path. Chelsea points to Krista's chest. "How does it feel to have on old man living in your boobs?" she asks.

"I think I can hear him wheezing like a pervert," says Amber. She snorts, trying to imitate the old cartoon heart-man.

"Come on, Krista," I say, pulling her over to my side so we can walk around them. "Just ignore them."

As usual after they've spewed out their venom, Chelsea

and Amber disappear. It's not hard for us to get to the cafeteria, grab some food and blend in.

After school, Krista walks me up to the main road. She never comes with me to pick up Annie because her mom likes her home before she has to leave for her shift at the hospital. We're about to say goodbye when Chelsea appears out of nowhere, her cellphone held up in her hand. She stops and clicks — one, two, three pictures of Krista, right in her face.

"Hey, it's the paparazzi," someone behind us calls.

Krista and I stand there, frozen, as Amber and a few other girls gather around Chelsea, laughing. Chelsea runs her thumb over her phone, showing them the shots. When she gets to the end they crack up and take off.

There was no flash, but Krista's face looks like there was.

"You okay?" I ask.

Krista nods and I'm glad to see that she can move.

"Why don't you come with me? We can all walk to your place together, then I'll take Annie home."

Krista shakes her head. "Can't. I'm alright. See you tomorrow."

I watch her walk off. People are still looking over at her. I can only imagine how she must feel. And when I think of Chelsea taking those pictures of Krista, I shudder. I don't know why. I just do.

I wanted to tell Chelsea that my heart used to be the size of a walnut. It really was, because, as incredible as it seems, I was a preemie. Being there with me, day after day, was what gave my mom the idea to take the nursing assistant's course. If I could turn my preemie heart into a cartoon it would have tiny delicate wings and it would be sleeping with a sweet face, totally unbothered by the world.

I can't believe that I once weighed three pounds and was the size of my dad's fist. But it's true. For two whole months I lay in an incubator, taking food in through a tube. My mom said I was so small that my leg bones were like the turkey wishbone we crack apart at my grandmother's on Thanksgiving.

But I don't dare tell anyone. If I did, they'd automatically wonder how I could go from that to this in just thirteen years. It's hard enough that people already look at me all the time, like something's wrong with me. Sometimes, I pretend they're not looking at me, but at some random girl that I'm not connected to. I'm someone else.

Something like this: the fattest girl in grade eight is in line with her tray. She's holding it out in front of her stomach, as if to hide herself. Everyone wants to see what the fat girl will put on her tray. For sure, it will be hamburgers and fries and soda, all the things that made the fat girl fat in the first place. The fat girl knows everyone is looking and putting two and two together and wondering why she is too stupid to know that those things are only going to make her fatter.

Why does she choose those things? Because she is determined to act as normal and unfat as possible. If everyone else can load their trays with those things, why can't she? Besides, she likes those things. Who doesn't? Show her one person in this school who would rather eat a salad than a hamburger and she'll run around the block ten times. How does the fat girl hold her face while she's holding her tray loaded with fatty foods? She holds it as light and bubbly as possible. Look closely and you might see the bubbles percolating up through her nose and into her brain, like the bubbles in a can of soda. Not a care in the world does this fat girl have.

She is so carefree, not even Tessa, sitting there eating her healthy homemade lunch, notices the other side. Only one person has noticed it: the lunch lady, the one who takes the orders and slops the burgers or lasagna or pork chops on the plates. Why does she notice? Maybe because she is big too. How does the fat girl know she notices? That's easy — she sees it in the lunch lady's eyes when she slides the plate over the stainless steel counter. Normally, she never looks up to see whose food she's serving. Except for when it's the fat girl. Then, the lunch lady looks — a quick, two-second look, her eyes hooded but her dark irises piercing the fat girl as strongly as if she'd reached over with her stainless steel spatula and stabbed her with it.

I did it again today, when Chelsea was taking my picture. I pretended it wasn't me being captured forever on her phone. Sitting there for her to post and share and send around the world. I have to pretend. Pretending is my fort, my arsenal. Without pretend, that click would have felled me like a bullet.

CHELSEA

I thought about the pictures on my phone like some disease while driving around with Tyler, until he had to snap his fingers in front of my face to get my attention. He didn't look too happy. I better not do that again.

I swear that the only thing keeping me going is the way Tyler looks at me. It's only been a few days but already I just count off the long, boring hours at school until I can be with him again. It's like torture, listening to teachers go on about stuff that happened hundreds of years ago. Or trying to get me to understand how a bunch of Xes and Ys make sense. I wish I could do like Tyler and just quit. But my mom would go ballistic. If I could think of something to do instead, I would quit. I wouldn't care about my mom. Like if I could work and get my own place. But who would rent a place to a thirteen-year-old?

I wonder what Tyler would say if I asked him if I could live with him. I'm going to try to work up the nerve. The thing is, I don't really ask him many questions. I made that mistake yesterday, when he left me in the car for a long time and went off without a pizza, and he didn't like it. He asked if this was the Spanish Inquisition, whatever that is. I can't risk him getting mad again. Not when he told me I'm the most well put-together thirteen-year-old he's ever met. He said I should be at modelling conventions, that a beauty like mine should be shared. Nothing that happens at school could top that. Who cares if I failed another math test or got a zero for that English essay about the poem?

Tyler got out of the car for a long time again tonight, and while I sat and waited, trying not to get too cold with the heater off, I sent the pictures to Amber and then deleted them. I thought about how, one day, I'll live in a place where there are no ugly fat people. There's way too many of them in my school and I hate having to look at them, especially Krista. I don't get how someone could let herself get that way. Doesn't she care what other people think? Maybe being fat just makes her dumb and she doesn't know how horrible she looks. Maybe if she could see herself the way people like me see her, she'd stay home and stop making an ugly place even uglier. Maybe that's what gave me this great idea that I'm going to talk to Amber about tomorrow. It can be our school project for the term. If only it could be marked. I'm sure it would get an A+.

CHAPTER FIVE

Friday morning, Krista and I walk to her locker first, like we always do before heading to mine. We see it at the exact same second — a huge picture of Krista's face, caught with her mouth open and her cheeks twisted as she was turning — and we stop dead. We suck in our breath and neither of us speaks.

Chelsea must have used one of the pictures she snapped of Krista the other day, then Photoshopped it to make Krista look like a monster. Even the tint of her skin is greenish. She and Amber must have snuck in early to hang it on Krista's locker. Under the huge picture they hung a sign that says, *Krista, the Goodyear Barbie,* in thick dark letters.

I bet they had the time of their lives.

Suddenly, Krista flings herself forward and begins tearing at the picture. It's hard — they used a thick roll of tape that covers all the edges. No matter how frantically Krista and I dig in our nails and pull, we can't get a grip. The whole time I can hear Krista sobbing.

I turn to look behind me and see that Chelsea and Amber and some other friends are walking up and down the hall, laughing really loud, not even trying to hide their joy. Then they start taking pictures of us tearing down the picture. And then one of them backs up and takes a picture of them taking a picture of us taking down a picture. I can't believe it. I listen to them laughing until I can't take it anymore. I run over to Chelsea and rip her phone out of her hands. Then I jump on it, smashing it to bits. It lets off a crackling noise under my feet, like a firecracker. I should stop then, but something makes me grab a handful of her hair. I yank harder than I've ever yanked anything in my life. It's the type of yank I might give if Annie were stuck in a burning room and I had to pull her out the window to safety. The type of yank I wish someone had given my dad to get him away from the flames of his vehicle.

Chelsea's friends bounce backward, afraid to get close. Next thing I know, the principal is grabbing hold of me and prying my fingers loose. He pulls me down the hall, holding me under the arm, as I twist backward to see what's happening to Krista. How could he leave her alone with those girls? But I can't see her. I can only make out a shape on the floor.

An hour later, I'm sitting in his office with my mom. It's the first time she's been out since the break, other than trying to meet me and Annie at the clinic. And the elevator is broken today, so she was forced to climb down six flights of stairs on crutches. It must have taken her forever just to get down to the taxi.

"So, young lady, what do you have to say for yourself?" asks Mr. Steinbrenner, our principal.

"Not much," I say. I'm looking down at my hands to make sure I'm not still holding any of Chelsea's hairs. I don't dare look at my mom.

"Tessa, look at Mr. Steinbrenner when he's speaking to you," she says, using her *I raised you right and you should know better* voice.

"Sorry."

"You know we have a zero-tolerance policy for violence at this school. No matter what set you off, I am forced to apply it. It isn't discriminatory."

"I know."

"Tessa, why did you go crazy like that?" asks my mom. "They tell me you had another girl on the ground."

I shrug.

"She may have been provoked, Mrs. Deane. The girl she attacked was part of a group that taped a picture up to her friend's locker. Is that right, Tessa?"

"Yes."

"A picture? Just a picture. For that you beat someone up? I can't believe that. Is that true?" asks mom.

I nod.

"Tessa, talk to me." My mom bangs my chair with her crutch to shake me up.

"Okay. It's true what he, I mean Mr. Steinbrenner, said. They taped a picture to Krista's locker. It was awful, Mom. It was all blown up and they wrote *Krista, the Goodyear Barbie* across the bottom. We were trying to tear it off and they were laughing. I snapped. That's it."

The three of us sit there, dead silent until finally Mr. Steinbrenner speaks. "I am taking that into account, Tessa. That and what your family has been through, with your father and all." My mom and I take a deep breath — no one ever talks about my dad in front of us. I didn't even know he knew.

"I'm suspending you for all of next week. Think about how you respond, Tessa. What Chelsea did was wrong, but so was your response."

I am already thinking. I'm thinking about the teachers who must have walked down the hallway this morning and seen the locker. Had they noticed? If they did, why didn't they do anything about it? What if they saw it and thought it was funny? Or maybe they thought it was giving Krista a message she needs to hear and chose not to get involved. Wasn't that wrong, too?

"Tessa?" My mom nudges me with her elbow.

"Yes, sir."

My mom struggles to her feet. We're about to leave when she turns back to Mr. Steinbrenner. "And the girl who put up the picture? She'll be punished too, I hope?" She doesn't look away. She pierces his eyes with hers. I wonder if she's thinking the same as me — that the picture on the locker was like an IED, something thrown together last minute and set to explode.

"Oh, don't you worry, Mrs. Deane, she will be. She most certainly will be. Her suspension will be for two weeks, maybe more."

Relief floods through me. I'll be safe for a little while, at least.

KRISTA

I looked like a character from a horror movie. If you could have seen my hand it would have held a dagger dripping with blood. When I touched the picture I got a shock, like it was electric. And when I ripped a strip off it it made me look even funnier. At least it must have been funny because I could hear laughing behind me. Funnier than when kids pee their pants or throw up in class, funnier than when girls get their periods and have brown spots on their jeans, funnier than when teachers come back from lunch with lettuce on their teeth. The funniest of all: me, Krista, the fat girl, captured like a pinup poster of a supermodel, plus plus plus-size, *The Goodyear Barbie*. Even my lovely dark hair twisting over my shoulders looked ridiculous, like it was trying to fool people into not seeing the rest.

Then it struck me: what if the picture wasn't Photoshopped? What if that was how I really looked? I stopped ripping. I stood back and took myself in. I barely noticed that Tessa was rolling around on the floor behind me, fighting with Chelsea. Everything faded — first sound, then sight. It was like nothing existed but me and the picture.

If I made a sound when I hit the ground I didn't hear it, although I'm sure a huge thud vibrated down the hall and into the chemistry lab, rattling the petri dishes. The next thing I knew I was lying on the bed in the nurse's office. I don't know how I got there and I don't want to know. I don't want to picture the team of people heaving and ho-ing. I don't want to think of all the kids lined up outside their lockers watching me pass by. I don't want to picture my shirt riding over the top of my jeans, exposing my rolls. Maybe more photos were taken. Maybe there are now enough pictures sitting in cellphones to cover my locker every day for the rest of the year. Or to splatter all over the Internet.

My dad came to get me. I bet when he walked down the hall people pointed and said he must be the Goodyear Barbie's dad — "Can't you tell?" It was the first time he'd ever had to pick me up from school. He said he'd nearly had a heart attack in his forklift when they paged him on the intercom. That hadn't happened since the day I was born.

In my head, I thought how appropriate that it should happen again the day I died.

I saw on *E!* that a gang of kids called the Bling Ring robbed Paris Hilton's house and stole thousands of dollars of stuff. They had a picture of the ringleader getting into her SUV, wearing a fur vest and high-heeled boots. She had huge sunglasses and tons of jewellery. She actually wore some of Paris's clothes to a night club, which is how she got caught. The whole thing was turned into a reality show on E! Even her trial. The day of the trial, the camera crew shot in their living room. It was full of carved statues that reached the ceiling. I don't get why someone like that needs to belong to the Bling Ring. And her mom's crying looked totally fake. My mom wouldn't have that problem. She'd rip my ears off, live.

What I did at school isn't getting me a TV show, but Tyler said it should. He said I should have a reality show about my life. It could show my transformation from nobody to somebody. He said the fight scene in the hall would have been great footage, with two girls rolling around on the floor. I didn't tell him all the details, like how Tessa wrecked my phone. I didn't tell him about the picture, either, and how Amber helped me print it up. He thinks we started fighting for no reason. I don't know why I didn't tell him. I probably could've. I think he'd find it funny. I loved it when he said he was glad she didn't leave any marks and that if she'd hurt my face he'd have killed her. He likes me to look perfect. When I told him about the suspension, he smiled and said it was cool. Now we could ride together for two whole weeks and that would make his days sweeter.

My mom was pissed off big time, even though I told her the other girl started it, which she did. She's never on my side, so I don't care. It was so funny when Krista saw what we did to her locker. She stood there staring for ages, her skin turning redder and redder. I know she couldn't believe that was her, but it was. I had to take pictures of her looking at it. That wasn't such a bad thing to do. I mean, it's not every day something exciting actually happens at school. It's usually all blah blah blah. School gave me the idea anyway, from that dumb poem we read where the fat girl finally learns how she looks and tries to change. That's what this was all about. This was my poem to her, but it was a picture instead.

The only thing I didn't expect was Tessa jumping on my back and ripping my phone out of my hands. Next thing I knew she was pulling my hair, yanking it like she thought it was all extensions. She jumped on my cell, smashing it to bits, and I knew my mom would kill me because I'd had to beg her to buy it for me. Then we were down on the ground, tumbling around like mud wrestlers. Lucky for her the principal pulled us apart. Tessa is so pathetic. She sits in the front of every class like there's something she can't miss. And she eats lunch with Krista and doesn't lose her appetite. She lives in the building beside Amber's, so I've seen her going in and out with her mom and sister. The three of them always look so happy together, all holding hands, like some sucky TV family.

Sometimes I think about how unfair it is that you can't

choose where you're born. Like, some people just get to be born in a place like that girl in the Bling Ring. And some people, like me, get to be born nowhere. Tyler says that's why we have to work harder at getting somewhere. He says when we get there we'll be even happier than they are.

CHAPTER SIX

On Tuesday I visit Krista for the first time since it happened. She's tucked up in bed in her pyjamas, like she's sick. A tray sits on her night table, holding a plate of toast and a bowl of red Jell-o. It reminds me of hospital food, which makes it seem even more like Krista is ill.

"How are you?" I say, pulling over a chair.

"How do you think?" she answers.

"Yeah, I know. Lame question. But I mean it. How are you doing?"

Krista hesitates for a few seconds, like she can't figure out how to answer me. Then she blurts out, "I've lost three pounds. I'm happy about that."

"That's great, but, like, are you okay — you know?" I don't want to say "in the head" because I don't want her to think that I think she's gone crazy.

"I'm fine. I'm just not eating much. I'm drinking though. Water. That's about it."

"But you need to eat something. You'll get sick if you

don't." I've never known Krista not to eat, no matter what.

"No, I won't. I feel better than ever. I'll keep feeling better too, the more I lose."

I don't know what to say. We've never really talked about her weight before. It's always been there between us, but we've tried to ignore it.

"Okay, then. I guess you know what you're doing."

"Yeah, I do."

Then we look at each other for a while, without talking. I thought we'd have so much to say, but that's not how it is. I thought we'd talk about Chelsea, but I don't want to say her name aloud and bring her into the room. In the end, Krista says she's tired and wants to sleep so I leave. I've only been there half an hour.

On the way home I think about my suspension and how it compares with what Krista is going through. Next week I'll go back to school but I'll still be the same person, only with a blemished record. I can't help thinking of that "Barbie Doll" poem again. Maybe Krista is hoping to transform herself like the girl in the poem did. I wonder why Ms. Bane chose it, with Krista in her class. Did she consider how it would affect her? Maybe she weighed the pros and cons and decided that it would help Krista in the end by giving those idiots in our class a new perspective on her. It would show them how it might feel to be teased and what the consequences might be. If that's the case, she made a huge miscalculation, one that Krista is paying for.

KRISTA

Last night, I looked out my window and felt like I could jump off the sill and fly away into the night, like Wendy in Peter Pan. That's because I feel light for the first time in ages. I haven't eaten a thing since breakfast Friday morning, three days ago, the day of the picture. Not a crumb.

All weekend my mom brought me trays of food, and when she came back to take them away not one thing had been touched. I could see her shrug and hear her sigh, even though she tried to suppress it. She hasn't lectured me yet, not really. She only mentioned school once, to tell me I'd have to go back. I know she wants to say more, but she's holding it in. I can see the words jamming up in her mouth, making her lips shake. I don't know how long we'll continue to play this game but the longer we do, the lighter I'll get.

The hunger is a hard rumble in my belly, as though a giant fist is scraping around in there, trying to excavate something. Maybe doing an archaeological dig to find old chicken bones and pizza crusts and make a record of how I became what I am. Or was. I'm not going to let my mother turn me back into what I was. I know what she's trying to do with her food: make up for years of letting me eat crap. She brings me: three-course meals covering the food groups — two scoops of mashed potatoes that look like perfect breasts, a strip of meat, a clump of corn and beans that are so shiny I wish I could thread them on a string, and a big glass of milk.

She doesn't know that I like the rumbly feeling in my

belly. It distracts me from other things, like the pictures in my head that I don't want to see. When my mind starts to drift there I can stop it by sending it down to my stomach. It's like I'm grabbing that rumbling fist with my mind and anchoring myself to it as it twists and turns in my gut.

Today, after my dad left for work, I took my second big step toward losing weight. I ordered some pills online: 90 Phentexplus. I had snuck my dad's credit card out of his wallet on the kitchen table when he was still sleeping and copied the number and expiry date. By the time the statement comes, I'll be too thin to care. And I can pay him back. I have birthday money saved up. I don't know why I never thought of doing this before.

Even though I can never go back to school, what happened there was a good thing, in a way. It gave me the kick I needed to take action. I felt so good clicking that "Order Now" button. I even asked for special delivery and made a notation that they should come tomorrow between one and two, when my mom will be sound asleep. The website had a long list of side effects. I glanced at them quickly but they didn't seem too terrible: sore stomachs and smelly gas and headaches, but not for sure — just maybe. To be fair, they should list the side-effects of *not* using them: constant humiliation, irreparable bruising to the ego, and irreversible loss of self-esteem.

I am so hungry, but I won't eat until those pills come. I'll spend the day listening to the rumble. It's low now, like a motor running out of gas way in the distance. Tomorrow, I will eat but just a bit. I'll let the pills do the rest.

CHELSEA

I'm getting so tired of my mom telling me what to do. I try to stay asleep so that I don't have to see her before she leaves for work, but she bangs around making noise on purpose. It's like it's killing her that I'm getting to sleep in when she can't. She hauls the vacuum cleaner and attachments out of the hall closet and crashes them against my bedroom door every morning, to give me a message. As if the whole house is filling up with dust just because I'm home.

I watch a show called *Make It or Fake It* where they take girls and try to turn them into supermodels. They have to have the right everything: hair, legs, cheekbones, eyes. Then they walk down a runway in a fashion show with real models and the audience has to guess which girls are just faking it. Sometimes, one of them ends up making it for real in the business. I know if I had a chance, I would, too. Why can't my mom get that and leave me alone? Only Tyler understands me. He says he wants to help me get out of here and make something of myself. Then I'll really leave my mom behind in the dust. She'll have to vacuum every day for the rest of her life just to breathe.

She told me that if I keep staying out so late at night she's going to wash her hands of me — whatever that means. It's not like I'm asking her for anything. I don't need to, now that I have Tyler. He even bought me a new cellphone when he thought I'd lost mine. Maybe that's why my mom's so angry all the time. I have Tyler and she has no one, not that she knows about him. Maybe she can sense it. She's had boyfriends herself but none of them stay. They can't stand the way she gets cranky with them. I'm not going to get that way with Tyler, no matter what. That's why I take so long to get ready. I have to make myself look perfect and polished and that takes time.

Before leaving, I kick the vacuum cleaner hose out of the way, then roll the machine down the hall closer to my mom's door. Let her vacuum. I'm not choking on dust. In Tyler's car, with the window down, nothing but fresh air is hitting my face.

CHAPTER SEVEN

My mom is getting her cast taken off today and I've gone with her, since I'm home anyway. When the doctor reveals her foot, the skin is white and rubbery, like a chicken. She says it's so itchy she could scratch right down to the bone, but the doctor says she shouldn't. He lets me look at the old x-rays and he doesn't make me feel dumb when he explains how the ankle is one of the most complex joints in the human body because it is where three bones meet: the fibula, the tibia, and the talus.

"Usually, it's the tibia that breaks. Sometimes, it's the fibula and even more rarely, the talus. But your mom's break involved both the tibia and fibula — something I rarely see." Then she stares at the spot for a full minute, as though it's a work of art.

She shows my mom the exercises she has to do to strengthen the muscles around her ankle bones. "You keep your mom in line and make sure she does them," she says, winking at me.

In the afternoon, I take the bus downtown to the

pharmacy to fill her prescription for anti-itch creme. The bus is full of old people with net shopping bags looped over their arms and homeless people in dirty jackets, their snoring heads rattling against the windows. Some older students who are obviously off to the university sit reading notes or snoozing over their backpacks. I wonder if I'll be one of them one day, memorizing long and complicated lists of bodily functions for important tests or falling asleep because I've been up all night studying.

I pick up the prescription and a list of stuff my mom gave me: toothpaste, soap, shampoo, menstrual pads, and aspirin. I don't like the way the cashier looks at me, like she's wondering why I'm at the store in the middle of the day when I should be in school. I can feel her making up the story of my life in her head as she scans my items. When she picks up the pads she even shoots me a sympathetic smile, like she thinks they're for me. I slap the money on the counter, grab the bag, and leave before she can call me "dear."

Next, I stop at The Bean Sprout Café to pick up my mom's paycheque. Karen and Matt have actually been paying her a portion of her salary while she's home, which is something my mom said no one else in this city would do. They're happy to see me and insist on filling me up with a smoothie and carrot cake. They also fill a take-home container with Three-bean Mexican Salsa Salad. The whole time I'm there I try to look into the back to see who replaced my mom. I know she'll want to know. She said no one is irreplaceable and if Karen and Matt have found someone good that could be it for her. But I don't think that's happened. They ask a million questions about my mom's foot and they're so relieved when I say the cast is off and she can start putting pressure on it that they high-five each other.

I can't stay longer because I have to bring my mom the stuff and then run up and meet Annie at school. I get off the bus at the stop beside the park, two blocks from home. A minute later, I'm passing the pizzeria when a car door opens and Chelsea jumps out. She stands in front of me with her hands on her hips and a crooked smile on her face. It's like she's been waiting in that car all week, just hoping I'd walk by, ready to pounce when I did. A few seconds later a guy comes out of the pizzeria. He looks way older than her, with long dark hair pulled straight back, so tight I can still see the comb tracks on his skull. He must be the delivery guy because he's holding a stack of boxes.

"This her?" he asks, grinning.

"Yeah," says Chelsea. Her word is like a secret command. The guy chuckles and says, "Okay." He puts the stack on the hood of the car and before I can move he's got me by the arms and is pushing me around the corner onto a quieter street.

Chelsea has followed us. She snatches my bag and rips open the box of pads. She flings them into the air, one by one, making them fly like little white pillows. Then she unscrews the lid of the aspirin bottle and sends the pills rolling into the gutter. She tucks the shampoo and soap into her jacket pocket. Next, she pulls out the tube of creme and twists off the cap. She squirts the creme onto the front of my jacket in the shape of an X. I twist to get away but the guy is holding me too tightly. Finally, she pulls out the Three-bean Mexican Salsa Salad and dumps it over my head. I can taste it as it drips into my mouth, sharp and vinegary.

"Eat that," she says. Then she holds up her sharp nails like she's about to hook them into my face.

At school, they tell you that if something bad happens

you should look for the nearest adult and ask for help. But the nearest adult is the one holding me down. I feel the pressure of his fingers deep in my bones. If they were x-rayed now they'd have black holes in them.

Suddenly, the guy says, "We gotta go, Chelsea. Now!" He lets go of me and they jump into the car and take off.

I put my head down and run, knowing I must look like a complete idiot with my hair dripping vinegar and beans stuck everywhere, rolling down my neck and into my shirt, crawling down my back like bugs.

I don't cry. I'm too stunned. I just need to get home and out of what I'm wearing. I need to jump into the shower and wash off.

When I enter the apartment, my mom is down on her hands and knees in the kitchen, scrubbing the corners behind the stove. She calls hello and I answer back without stopping. I run straight to the bathroom and lock the door. I can hear my mom asking me if everything is all right as I peel the vinegar-soaked clothes off and shove them into the hamper.

"I'm fine," I call out.

In the shower, I gasp when I see the bruises on my arms. Four brown dots and one bigger one, for his thumb, on the underside. I have to empty the drain protector three times. It keeps filling with bits of bean and onion and tomato that are flushing out of my hair.

I'll have to think of something to tell my mom when she asks where the stuff from the pharmacy is. I hate lying to her, but if I tell her the truth she'll call the police. I know she will. And that would just make things worse with Chelsea. This way, she'll feel like she paid me back for breaking her cellphone and pulling her hair.

Besides, what would the cops do? They're always crawling around this neighbourhood looking for something or other, usually drugs. They catch people dealing in the back parking lot or break up fights where kids have knives. Every now and then a gun goes off and my mom says so much for gun control. What's the chance that the cops are going to make my case top priority? "Let's see: drug dealer or guy who holds girl getting attacked by Three-bean Mexican Salsa Salad?" Anyway, I'd just have to see that guy again, maybe pick him out of a lineup. Just the thought of him makes me shudder.

I wash the greasy X off my jacket the best I can, take a deep breath, and walk into the kitchen wrapped in a towel. It isn't hard to make my eyes tear up.

"Mom?" I say.

"Yes, honey."

"Oh mom, I'm so sorry. I left the bag on the bus. I feel terrible."

"Oh, Tessa. Is that why you were hiding in the bathroom?"

I nod and my mom walks over and throws her arms around me, pulling me close. Her chin settles on the top of my head. All I can think of is the vinegar — will she smell it? But she doesn't. She holds me for a long time and for a few minutes I forget about the five black bruises on my arm.

Now I know that my appetite was my enemy. It was always looming over me, like a monster, making me want to eat more. But the pills are shrinking it, turning it from a monster into a mouse. I can pick and nibble at the stuff my mom brings me and that keeps her happy.

She brings me breakfast when she comes home from her shift and wakes up early to cook dinner before heading off. It's usually something my dad just has to heat up, something that actually sat in a pot and bubbled on the stove, like a stew. I have a few bites: a chunk of carrot and potato and one lump of meat. That's all I need, thanks to my pills.

It's only been a few days but I wonder if my dad misses our routine. Is he out there resisting the temptation to pull a flyer out of the stack? I think he must be. I haven't heard the doorbell ring.

Today when my mom came home she sat in the chair beside my bed and took my hand. She started talking but my mind drifted. I couldn't focus. I tried to, but her words kept floating away on a bubble. Every now and then I caught one, words like *eat* and *food*, and it almost made me laugh. I knew she was here for one purpose: to get me to eat again. But I don't know why she's trying to send me right back to where I was before. Doesn't she get that *before* was not a good place to be? *Before* is what landed me on that locker, looking like some monster from a horror show.

When she asked me what would happen if I didn't go back to school, what would happen to my future, I kept my mouth shut. I didn't want to tell her there's only one thing that matters: my pills. They are easy to swallow, they have no taste, and they go into my bloodstream and through my nervous system and make me believe I'm not hungry.

What more could I ask for?

The minute I saw her walking toward us, I knew I had to tell him. I wanted him to see just how strong I could be and how much better I am than girls like her.

We'd just come back from some deliveries and Tyler was picking up another stack of boxes. I was waiting in the car when I saw her. She was wearing her ugly black jacket, the one with no shape. Little Black Riding Hood, clutching her shopping bag and walking along as if nothing bad could happen to her. She even had an I-gotta-get-home-to-Mommy look on her face.

Well, you know what happened to Little *Red* Riding Hood. Her walk through the woods didn't go that well. Tyler knew right away when he came outside and I pointed at Tessa. That's another thing I love about Tyler — I don't have to tell him much. He gets me. He grinned wide, like something big was about to happen. I love the way he walked up behind Tessa so confidently. He was a great big bad wolf.

By the time I held up my hands to scratch her, Tyler's eyes were wide with excitement. But I changed my mind. I had worked on my nails for hours, polishing and filing, capping them with fake tips. Scratching Tessa would only ruin them. So I didn't do it. I could see Tyler's face fall and his mouth get hard. I hoped he'd still let me ride with him. He let go of her and we got into the car. The pizzas would be cold in their boxes and Tyler's boss might yell at him, which always made him crazy.

In the car, he said he could see what had happened as a scene in a movie. Then his mood changed and he turned quiet. Finally, he asked me if I realized he could be in big trouble if the girl squealed. "I put myself out on a limb for you, Chelsea," he said. "You know that, don't you? A big limb. I mean, you're worth it. I don't mind doing it, but you might owe me one day. You know that, right?"

I nodded. I'd do anything for Tyler. He didn't need to ask.

CHAPTER EIGHT

As I walk toward Krista's on Sunday, I picture her sitting up in bed with a tray of food. It will be a full-course meal, lasagne, salad, roll with butter, milk, and another bowl of Jell-o with whipped cream plopped on top. Krista will be eating, her knife and fork busy in her hands. Her mouth will be rimmed with food and crumbs will be covering her pyjama top. Maybe she'll be so full she'll offer me the Jell-o, which I'll accept because I love Jell-o, although I do find it gross when I think how it's made of crushed cow bones.

But that's not how it is. Krista is rolled in a ball, her back to the door. She doesn't unroll when I walk in and whisper her name. I think she might be sleeping, until I see that her eyes are open. She doesn't blink when I walk around her bed, like she doesn't even see me.

"How's it going?" It's another dumb question, but what else can I say? Her shoulder shrugs slightly, so I know she can hear me.

I wait a while and then say, "Hey, my mom got her cast

off. She's almost walking like a normal person again." I don't tell Krista about Chelsea. Somehow, it doesn't seem like the smart thing to do. When Krista still doesn't talk, I pull out a deck of cards.

"Wanna play?"

Krista's head turns toward me, then her body follows. She moves slowly but eventually she's sitting up.

"You deal," she says and relief flushes through me. We play crazy eights for an hour and I don't mention food once, or school. Who am I to burst Krista's bubble? I can see why she wants to stay home. She's probably never felt safer in her life. There's no one around to point at her and snicker or call out nasty things, like, "How many Big Macs did you have for breakfast?" Whenever that happened, she'd drop her eyes to the floor, like she was ignoring the comment or trying not to attract attention. Afterwards, she'd walk with her books clutched to her chest like a shield. I had gotten used to her looking a bit scared all the time. But this Krista, slapping her cards down, has no worry lines on her face. She's like the Krista I remember from all the way back in kindergarten, except for the dark bags under her eyes and the way she gags and holds her stomach when she moves too fast.

Eventually, Krista's mom comes in carrying her dinner on a tray. It's pasta with salad, just like I imagined. Krista surprises me by picking up the salad, spearing a piece of lettuce, and putting it in her mouth. While she continues eating, munching on cucumbers and carrots, I take my chance and jump in.

"Hey, I'm going back to school tomorrow. I hope you're going to come with me."

"Oh, Krista. Isn't that a good idea? The two of you could go in together," says Krista's mom, stopping at the door.

"No way."

"But why not, Krista?" I ask. "Nothing's going to happen. They wouldn't do anything again and Chelsea won't even be there until next week." For three days I've been trying to erase the image of Chelsea standing over me with her nails inches from my face.

"It doesn't matter. I'm not going back there. Not tomorrow. Not ever."

"I wish you'd stop saying that. Tessa, I've tried many times. Maybe you can get through to her." Krista's mom sighs and leaves the room.

"Your mom's right, Krista. You can't *not* go to school." Krista shrugs and puts down her fork. She hasn't touched the pasta.

"Sure I can. Watch me."

Last time my dad came home he told me about girls' struggle to go to school in Afghanistan. Some men would throw stones, or burn their schools down. But the schools kept reopening and girls kept going. They couldn't let the bad guys win. I know it's not the same as Krista's story, but I wish she'd keep fighting.

"But you can't let them win. If you don't come back, that's what you're doing. Then they go on to high school and you don't. How is that fair? You didn't do anything wrong."

"I'll do school somewhere else, or at home."

"But what about me? You won't know anyone at another school and home is no fun."

We sit in silence for a while. I think about some of the women I've seen in Karen and Matt's Renaissance Art book, round and fleshy, surrounded by angels and fluffy clouds. Krista reminds me of them. Changing for gym, Krista always hides in a toilet stall, but what if she knew that at one time, her body would have been seen as beautiful? Maybe I'll even see if Karen and Matt will let me take that book home next time I babysit. One guy, Rubens, was even famous for painting chubby women.

But if I show her those pictures, she'll know I'm aware of her size. It might even seem like I've been thinking about it for years, making comparisons between her and other people.

Maybe, in a weird way, what Chelsea did just turned Krista into her real self — someone who feels fat. Maybe this shut-down has been lurking just below the surface for years. With me, she could just bounce along, pretending it didn't matter. But that picture made it real, something she couldn't ignore. And she knows I can't ignore either.

"Bye, sweetie. Goodbye, Tessa. Thanks for dropping by and thanks for trying." Krista's mom waves from the door, but Krista doesn't say goodbye back. She just closes her eyes, like she's shut off. I wait a few minutes, then say goodbye too. It seems like the only thing to do.

I like to pretend I'm a preemie, lying peacefully in my fragile sleep, half connected to the world — nothing but bones and quiet organs, with a layer of paper-thin skin covering the whole thing. Then I tuck myself into the tightest ball and shrink my mind to the size of a grape. I picture my little limbs as thin as new sticks. Even my breath grows shallow, as though my lungs are the size of peanuts. There are no pictures of the world in my head because I haven't opened my eyes yet. There are just swirly images of light and colour, like a psychedelic screen-saver.

I tried to get there today but a headache had wrapped around my forehead tight as a rubber band. I didn't even realize that Tessa had come in until she was sitting two feet from my face, bubbling away about this and that.

I watched her mouth open and I knew she was talking. Poor Tessa — she doesn't know how useless all that chatter is, how it hangs dead in the air between us. It took a minute to hook into her words. *School.* She was talking about going back to school. Nausea roiled through my stomach. School is so far away for me now. It is small, the size of a Monopoly building. Nothing matters right now except the pain in my head and stomach.

I could hear the thumping of my mom's heartbeat when she came near me. Maybe she was thinking about all the kids in the world who would love to have a proper meal delivered to them. Maybe it was the thought of the waste that made her slam the tray on my desk a little harder than usual, sending a stabbing pain into my head.

When she was gone, I stared at the plate. Like a photo in a textbook, each food group was represented. The lettuce was almost white, with just a hint of green, and topped with shredded carrot and cucumber. Salad was good for me and it wouldn't make me blow up. So, I lifted my fork and speared some. I raised it to my mouth. It would be the first food to pass my lips since dinner yesterday. Those pills really work. I have zero appetite.

Maybe one day I'll forget how to chew. My mom says lots of moms think they'll have to teach their babies how to drink the milk, but it's not like that. The babies are born making a sucking motion with their tiny mouths — it's called the survival instinct.

CHELSEA

Last night, before driving me home, Tyler pulled into a parking lot behind a closed superstore, the kind where people buy lumber and pipes and stuff. We had one pizza left over and no idea whose it was supposed to be. There was no address on the slip. His boss hadn't called him to say an angry customer was waiting for it. So Tyler said it must be fate, the pizza was ours. It was only a medium — all-dressed. I had one piece and Tyler had three. He said he likes the way I eat, taking little bites. Some girls gobble their food like pigs, which really turns him off.

He said a girl has to be aware of how she looks at all times and that some girls forget that. My mom is always telling me I spend too much time in front of the mirror, but she's wrong. It's more like she doesn't spend *enough* time there. If she did, she'd see that she should dye her hair and do something about her wrinkles.

She may not have been kidding about washing her hands of me, though. She used to wait up until I got in but she hasn't been doing that lately. And she used to save me some supper in the fridge but she's stopped doing that, too. We don't do anything together anymore and we barely speak. When I was little we'd watch cartoons and she'd let me play with her hair. I'd sit on the back of the sofa with a box of pins and barrettes and comb her hair up in crazy ways. She'd laugh at herself in the bathroom mirror after. But that was ages ago.

It's like my whole world is now two places: my apartment and Tyler's car. One I can't wait to leave, the other I can't wait to step into. In each one there are ways I need to behave, and in one of them, I'm getting it completely wrong. But I'm getting it right in the one that counts, at least.

CHAPTER NINE

This morning, my mom's hibiscus plant is in full bloom. Five reddish-pink flowers have blossomed among the leaves, each petal bigger than my thumb. The trumpet-shaped flowers are so perfectly formed, you'd think a master sculptor made them. I wish I could show the plant to Krista. I want her to see this beautiful thing and tell her that if someone tried for a million years, they'd never be able to make something so perfect. It's like those orchids that grow in the rain forest — ones I've seen in a book about Costa Rica. They sprout up through the muck and the mud and spring open, pink and purple and gold. I want Krista to see those too. I don't know why, but I think they'd help her.

My mom tries to be extra cheerful saying goodbye, as though it's just any other day and not my first day back after a one-week suspension. "Chin up," she says. But that's the worst advice. Chin down works better. Even though Chelsea won't be there, her friends will. I'll keep my eyes on the floor and try to stay invisible.

Walking there, my stomach flips over every time I think about me and Chelsea tumbling around on the dusty floor, her hair in my fist. And then I see her face, inches away from my own on the street. I can't let my fear show because Annie is walking beside me. I try to laugh as she babbles on about whatever, but I wonder if she can tell it's fake.

After last night, I am wondering a lot of things about what Annie knows.

My mom called me into the living room after Annie was asleep to show me something. The day before, she'd been vacuuming under Annie's bed when she sucked out a bunch of Annie's drawings. We sat on the sofa and flipped through them.

Annie had been drawing my dad's accident with the IED. Picture after picture showed an army truck flying up in the air, flames bursting out under it. Then there were body parts — heads, legs, arms, torsos — flying off in all directions. Some of the drawings had arrows pointing to the parts, beside which Annie had written, *dad's head* or *dad's arms*. Mom and I didn't know what to say. We didn't talk much about my dad when Annie was around. She was only two when he died. But she'd obviously heard more than we thought.

"Why now?" my mom kept asking. But I had no answers.

"I'm going to call her school and make an appointment with a counsellor," she said finally. "I'll bring these with me."

The last thing Annie needs now is to be scared about me getting hurt too.

I say goodbye to Annie at her school and turn back toward my own. I don't look up. I don't want to see who's around me. I think of my dad, who hadn't known what was waiting for him around the corner. He said a soldier has to sleep with one eye open, that he has to be aware of every sound, every flutter, every smell. I try to do that now.

My first surprise is when a bunch of girls standing at the top of the stairs, girls that I barely know, say, "Hey, way to go last week" and "Good for you, she deserved it." Later in the day, girls who have never looked at me twice are suddenly high-fiving me in the hallways. Even a few guys nod in my direction. It's all a bit strange. No one asks about Krista, though. It's like her part of the story didn't happen. I keep waiting for Chelsea's friends to approach me, but they're dispersed, as if they're under some kind of official ban.

At lunch I sit in the back at the loner table and face the wall. A few of the loner kids smile at me. They're even lower down in the pecking order than I am. I usually have Krista, at least. I look around at them and wonder why they're here. If I'm going to be eating with them from now on, I should try to get to know them.

I suddenly remember a picture my dad showed me when he was on leave, the year before he was killed. In it, he was sitting cross-legged on the ground with one of his army buddies, the two of them grinning ear to ear under their helmets. Lots of little kids were sitting in their laps and hanging off their backs. Some were laughing but most looked pretty serious. It was taken at an orphanage in the centre of a village that my dad's unit was patrolling. He told me most of the kids had lost their parents. Some were there because their parents couldn't feed them. Some of the girls were there because they had no males in the house, which made it hard to protect them. He and his friend used to bring the kids candy bars. He said they didn't fight over them like you'd think. There was a pecking order there, too, but my dad made sure they all got something, even if they had to share.

I pull some chips out of my lunch, split open the bag, and place it in the middle of the table. Then, I smile around at my four lunchmates. "Help yourselves," I say. No one wants to be first, until this kid reaches out and takes a chip. He smiles at me and stutters, "Th-th-thanks."

"No problem," I say. "Take more."

The others join in and I think of that picture again. Was it on him when he died, or is it safe in a locker somewhere? Maybe his friend's, the man in the picture. The two men who came to the house to tell us my father was dead said it would be easy for my mom to find out who was with him, if she wanted to speak to anyone, but so far she hasn't made any move to do so. She always says she wants to remember him as he was before, in his pre-army days. The trouble is, she has the most of that before-time to remember. There's only five years for me and none for Annie.

It would be good to have that picture back.

Every day now, when my dad is at work and my mom is sleeping, I creep out of bed and wander to the bathroom. I take a bath, hidden under mountains of bubbles. I like lying there with my eyes closed, the warm water surrounding me, feeling like I'm floating. I stay in there so long my skin puckers. When I get out of the water, I stand on the scale and weigh myself. I love the way the red arrow is a little farther down each time.

One day after school a bunch of kids blocked me in the hallway. They were holding up a big green garbage bag, its bottom corners cut off. I thought they were going to pull it over my head and try to suffocate me, but that would have been better than what they did do. Hey, Crisco, *one of them said.* We made you an extra pair of underpants, in case you can't hold it all in. *Someone else said,* We'd help you try them on, but we'd have to lift you first. *And another voice,* We could go get the football team to help out or borrow a crane. *And another,* But it would so be worth it. *Then the janitor appeared and they ran.*

The more the red arrow moves down, the more chance that stuff will never happen again.

Tyler has plans to travel all around the world. Once his pizza empire is established here he's going to take it right across the continent, from Vancouver to Miami, and then he's going to keep going across the ocean to all the big cities of Europe, like London, Paris, and Rome.

I wanted to ask if he'd take me with him because it sounded so exciting. Maybe we'd stay in luxury suites and have champagne and chocolate for breakfast. We'd bathe in one of those deep Jacuzzis, the kind with marble steps and gold taps. I'd pour sweet-smelling stuff into the water from fancy bottles. I wouldn't have to do anything except be with Tyler and look good. We could swim in one of those heart-shaped pools, the kind that has a bar on the side. Or maybe Tyler would own a yacht and we could sail from place to exciting place.

The thought of Tyler going off somewhere without me is too hard to take. If he left me here alone in this dump with no one to talk to but my mom I'd die. We have less and less to say to each other. Each day with her is the same. She gets up, goes to work, comes home, eats dinner, watches TV, and goes to bed. Sometimes, when I'm heading out the door, I look back at her and call goodbye, but she barely nods her head. Her eyes are fixed on the screen, like she's a zombie.

When I'm on the road with Tyler, I'll send her postcards so she can see how well I'm doing and how far I've travelled. She can add them to the pile of cards she gets from my half-brothers. They send her one every year on her birthday, just like she does for them. They never say much. Their lives seem as boring as hers.

CHAPTER TEN

If Krista knew how well it's going at school and how Chelsea and her gang have been disarmed, she'd come back. She doesn't need to know that no one asked about her again today. Or that there's still a tape outline of the picture on her locker. When she comes back I'll scrub it off somehow. I even know who I can ask for help — Paul, the guy who stutters. We had lunch together today. He's pretty funny. He's seen every science fiction film known to mankind and has a way of relating them to the food people bring for lunch. He said my three-pickle sandwich could've been in *Soylent Green*. It's an old movie set in the future (actually only about 12 years from now) when there's no food left anywhere on earth and people are starving. The only thing they eat is green mysterious stuff made by a big corporation. He said he didn't want to give too much away, in case I ever watch the movie. I was afraid he was going to ask me over to watch it today. How weird would that have been, to explain I couldn't come watch a movie about people starving because I was going to visit my best friend who is starving herself?

As I pass the guidance office on my way out, I glance at the pictures about anorexia and bulimia; they have tips on how to tell if you or a friend might have an eating disorder. But nothing on those posters prepares me for what I see when I get to Krista's. She looks so different. Her face is pale and drawn and her hair is clumpy with grease.

"Hey, Krista. People are on your side. Everyone wants you back," I say.

"Yeah, sure."

"You think I'm just making that up? I'm not. It's true."

"Yeah, sure."

She doesn't look at me, not once, and her voice is like a scratch. I know the old Krista is in there somewhere. I just have to pull her out. I have a sudden image of Krista ice skating on the outdoor rink ringed with pine trees, on the river. She's pirouetting, her hands high above her head, and laughing. I'm trying to do the same but my picks catch the ice and I land on my butt. The two of us hug and laugh, our jeans crusted with snow, our toes numb with cold.

Krista's mom brings us a plate of healthy snacks, cut-up apples and cheese and a heap of pistachios, but Krista won't even look at it. Her mom gives me a look at the door that says, Please try to get her to eat some — a little nudge with her chin toward the plate. She's already in her nursing uniform.

I decide the best thing I can do is eat some of the food myself. I chew slowly, showing Krista how good the apple is — sharp and crisp, just how I like them. A few of the pistachios are black inside, so I throw them into the garbage beside the bed. It's piled high with tissues. I wonder if she's been crying but I don't know if I should ask her. We used to tell each other everything, or at least I thought we did. Then I realize that I never told Krista what Chelsea and her boyfriend did to me. If I expect Krista to open up and be honest with me, maybe I have to do that with her. It's worth a try.

"Chelsea and her boyfriend attacked me," I blurt out.

"What? What are talking about?" She winces as though even talking hurts.

"They got me for, you know, fighting with her that day."

"What happened?"

"They stopped me on the street. I was coming back from the store. He held me and she dumped the stuff in my bag all over me."

"Oh my god, that's awful. Are you okay?" Krista's hand snakes out along her covers toward the plate. I try not to stare at it.

"Yeah, I'm fine — now. It was pretty bad, though. I had bruises. I haven't told anyone, not even my mom. You're the only one who knows."

Krista touches a piece of apple. "I don't know what to say. I'm sorry."

"It's not your fault. Anyway, the thing is, she hasn't come back to school yet. And her friends are all lost without her. None of them have said anything to me. I'm sure they're going to leave us alone. Maybe they regret that picture."

"Don't," Krista yells, her voice raw and mean. "Not the picture." She places her hands over her ears.

"Sorry. I just meant . . . I wanted you to know you can come back."

"No, I can't," Krista answers, uncovering her ears. "It's not just her. It's everyone. They all saw it. Everyone. You don't get it. Stop trying, Tessa." She pushes the plate away and turns her back on me.

I stare at the mound on the bed that is Krista, my best friend. She clearly wants me to leave. She has pulled all her sheets and blankets around her like a fortress. I'm just about to get up when I notice a bulge between her mattress and box-spring. I bend closer and see a small bottle. I bend even closer and see pills inside, white with blue flakes. Are they pain killers, sleeping pills? Would she tell me if I asked?

I know she won't turn around again, so I reach down and turn the bottle, quietly. The label says Phentermine 30mg. I've never heard of Phentermine and I have no idea what it's for. The bottle looks official, so why is she hiding it? Just then I hear her mom's footsteps coming down the hall. I quickly tuck the bottle back into its hiding place, pull the sheet over it, and say goodbye.

Tessa wants to pretend we're in this together, but we're not. She's never heard someone say, Hey Krista, can you lie down under the window so we can land on you next time we have a fire drill? Or, Hey Krista, I hear Big Mac is looking for love. Give him a bite. She's never sat down in the bus and watched her thighs spread out so that whoever is sitting beside her moves over a few inches or flinches and turns toward the window like she's full of germs. She's never seen kids hold their noses like she smells, even though she showers every morning with peach soap and shampoo that smells like lemons.

I could tell Tessa wanted to devour everything on the plate. But she held back, for my sake. I wanted to tell her not to. It doesn't matter. She can fill herself up as much as she wants to. The pills are filling me up in a better way. Too bad they make me feel so crappy.

CHELSEA

Lately, I've been riding with Tyler until midnight. He stops between deliveries a lot, doing what he calls his side business. He still doesn't let me get out of the car with him because he says it's his job to protect me. He told me it's nothing to worry about. It's just his way of making extra money. How is he supposed to save enough to open his pizza chain if he doesn't do extra? The tips aren't enough. I can tell what size of tip Tyler's gotten by how he acts when he gets back in the car. If it's a good one he'll be smiling. He'll lean over really close and say, Good one, Baby. When he calls me baby I melt inside. His face comes so close I can feel the heat on his lips, but he never kisses me. He made up a game where I take the pizza to the door instead of him. He said I'd get better tips, especially if a guy answered. And he was right. Tyler said the same guy who always gives him two bucks gave me five. Once, during the day, an old lady answered and asked why I wasn't in school. That made Tyler kind of nervous so he said I better just deliver to places he knew. We didn't want some old geezer spoiling our fun.

Sometimes, I picture Tyler pulling into a dark spot away from all the buildings. I want him to lean over and undo my blouse, button by button. He'd see that I'm wearing a pink lacy bra that I stole last week just for him. I want him to run his fingers up my thigh and under my skirt. Then he'd feel the lacy thong I stole to go with it. But I know I'm lucky he's not all over me. It means he respects me. And treats me so well, except when I do something he doesn't like, like talking too long at the door if I make the delivery. He tells me not to and I try not to, but if someone keeps blabbing what am I supposed to do?

CHAPTER ELEVEN

TESSA

My mom went to Annie's school today to talk about Annie's pictures. She said the psychologist laid them out on her desk and shuffled them around like she was making a collage. My mom studied her face, trying to figure out if she should be worried. Finally, the psychologist said that Annie had a lot of talent, which surprised my mom because it wasn't what she was expecting.

"Don't worry. I can see how the pictures would be disturbing to you, given what happened to your husband," she said when she saw my mom's face.

It turns out they have a file on Annie and in it is a detailed account of my dad's death. I suppose my school has a similar file on me. That way, if either of us shows signs of odd behaviour, the paper will tell them why. I remember Mr. Steinbrenner telling my mom that he knew about my dad and now I know how. The explosion happened when I was in grade three, at another school. That piece of paper must have followed me from school to school. I wonder if it will follow me to college, like some weird piece of identification.

"But should I be worried?" my mom asked. "Are Annie's drawings a sign of some deep, dark trauma brewing in her little brain?" I can't imagine it. Whenever I think of Annie, it is always of her smiling. Karen and Matt call her "little sprite" and they don't mean the soft drink. They mean a little elf or fairy, although the drink works too because it's bubbly, just like my sister.

"No. The drawings are most probably Annie's way of working out what happened to her dad. She was so young at the time. Do you talk about it much?"

When my mom said no, the psychologist nodded. "Then Annie has had to piece the accident together by herself. The pictures are her way of doing that."

All this time, we've been trying not to talk about the incident so we wouldn't put scary images into Annie's mind; but the more we didn't say, the more her mind filled with images anyway, ones she had to make up herself. The trouble is, Annie was so young when our dad died, she doesn't have any memories of him. She has to rely on us and we haven't given her much.

"So, what we have to do," says my mom, "is encourage Annie to keep drawing but tell her the details about Dad. And we also have to convince her to bring her pictures out from under the bed. As long as they're in the dark, they're too powerful."

"Maybe we could add them to her art gallery," I say. "With Annie's permission, of course."

"That would be perfect."

After supper, we talk to Annie and my mom explains exactly what happened to my dad. Annie imagined my dad's body flying apart but it wasn't like that. He was still alive after the explosion. They flew him to an army hospital in Germany right away, for surgery, but he died soon after. He'd lost a lot of blood and there was shrapnel lodged all over his body.

It's hard for Mom to talk about and I get that. I prefer to remember my dad in his security guard uniform. It was navy blue, with a gold "Security" tag pinned to his chest pocket. That's the job he did before joining the army, in an office building downtown. He had to sit and stare at screens all night long, making sure no one was breaking in. The worst thing he ever caught was a homeless man sleeping in the underground parking garage. He said the man appeared as a black blob in the security camera. My dad went down to check it out, holding out his flashlight like a gun. The guy was no older than my dad, dirty from head to foot, rolled up under a big piece of cardboard. My dad was supposed to kick him out but he said he couldn't do it. It was freezing outside, and what harm was the guy doing? So, my dad looked the guy straight in the face and said, "Okay, Buddy, as long as you're gone by six." That's my strongest memory of my dad.

We have fun putting up the pictures, even though it's weird to see flying soldiers lying beside cows that are peacefully munching grass. Or a tank on fire amidst sunny mountains and deep blue lakes. Annie gets right into it, rolling the tape on the back side so it won't show. She knows exactly where she wants to hang each one, as though she's putting them up in an order that makes sense to her. My mom smiles even when she's handling the most gruesome picture to let Annie know there's nothing wrong with thinking and imagining.

"Pictures can't hurt us," she says. "Sometimes they can even make us feel better."

I think about the bloated and twisted picture of Krista. It didn't help her — it hurt her, badly. But maybe that's because it wasn't really a picture of her. It was a picture of how Chelsea saw her — inflated and ugly. The psychologist said pictures could help heal wounds. That means there might be another picture out there that could help Krista by neutralizing the last one and taking away its power. I just have to figure out what it is. And I have to do it fast. Today, I googled *Phentermine* in the computer lab. I can't believe what I saw. It's a diet drug. There are dozens of sites. Some of them call it a miracle drug and show before-and-after pictures of people who have taken it and lost tons of weight. Others describe it as a nightmare. The pills have all kinds of side effects, some of them pretty serious, like heart attacks.

The way that bottle is hidden in her bed tells me Krista's parents have no idea she's taking them. So many of the sites have easy order options, it wouldn't have been hard for her to get them on her own.

In fact, I might be the only person in the world who knows, apart from Krista.

My parents took me to the hospital, propped up between them. My dad had two dark circles under his eyes and every time he looked at me his eyes misted up. The way he said "Good luck" at the hospital door scared me. It was as if I was having an operation. But it was a regular appointment. I don't know why my mom made it — I'm not sick. I'm just sick of being fat.

The sign on the doctor's door said, " Dr. Jane Hatrioff:

Nutritionist: Adolescent Specialist." As we waited I thought of ways to disguise how I was feeling. I wouldn't mention the pain in my head, which is deepening every day, the band pulled tighter. I wouldn't say that my stomach burns all the time and that, on top of the burning, I feel like I'm being stabbed. Sometimes, the stabbing wakes me up at night and then I stay awake for hours, tossing and turning. I wouldn't tell her that yesterday the pains in my stomach moved further up into my chest, like something was trying to stab my heart.

Doctor Hatrioff asked me a ton of questions about my eating habits, going back a month. It was like a before-and-after profile: my food intake before the "incident" and my food intake after it. She looked at the list and shook her head and said a bunch of stuff about diet and nutrients.

I didn't like being there. I didn't like someone saying the words *diet* and *weight* right to my face. I didn't like being under the fluorescent lights that buzzed like mosquitoes. I didn't like putting on a hospital gown and lying on the table. I didn't like a stranger looking at me and touching me, taking my pulse and blood pressure, listening to my breathing, and drawing blood from my arm.

My eyes drifted to the pictures of skinny girls on the walls, their rib cages like xylophones. She filled in some charts and forms, explaining about vitamins and minerals and the importance of protein over carbohydrates, about good fats and bad fats. When she filled in a meal plan and asked if I understood, I nodded, even though I was barely listening. The band around my head had tightened so hard my skull felt like it was going to burst.

All I wanted was for my mom to take me home. I wanted to crawl back in bed and block out the world. I forgot just how much I hate to be seen.

CHELSEA

Tyler said he knows somebody in the modelling business who will take me on for sure. He's going to introduce me to him soon, at a party. If it works out, maybe I won't go back to school for long. I'd love that. I don't even want to go back next week. Tyler said he's going to miss me, but he'll come pick me up if he can. I can't wait to see people's faces when he does. If the car didn't have a giant pepperoni pizza mounted on top, I could pretend it was his.

My mind started racing to what I was going to wear to the party. I don't have anything and Tyler will expect me to look good. That's not going to be easy with the crap I have in my closet. It must be amazing to have nothing but beautiful things to wear. To be able to close your eyes and put your hand into your walk-in closet, grab the first thing your hand touches, and have it be perfect. Every morning I have to rummage through heaps of ugly stuff to pull out something nice. I try to change it up so it doesn't look like something I've worn before but it's hard. There's only so many ways you can roll up a shirt or layer it with other stuff.

Maybe if I had a dad he'd spoil me, but I've never met my dad. For all I know, he might even be rich, like Kim Kardashian's. Maybe he has a yacht that he sails all over the world in. But where would my mom have met someone like that? And why wouldn't she be chasing him down for money?

On the other hand, if my dad were around that would make it harder for me to hang out with Tyler. Tyler even said that he likes that I don't have a dad. That way he has no competition and no big authority figure telling me I can't hang out with him. I haven't told him about my mom and the fact that she doesn't like it either. But I guess he's right — a dad would be worse. A dad wouldn't want to see his little girl with an older guy. If he were a big, strong dad they might end up in a fist fight over me. There I'd be, standing back and watching the two most important men in my life fighting over me. I wouldn't know who to cheer for.

CHAPTER TWELVE

I spend the whole weekend trying to think up a plan to help Krista. It has to be something I can do myself, without any parents. I don't let anything distract me, until late Sunday night when the doorbell rings.

I hear my mom open the door and a man says, "Hi, Sam."

"Johnny?"

"In the flesh."

"What are you doing here?"

"Just passing through."

The only Johnny I know is my dad's brother. He lives in Seattle and I've only met him once, way back when I was little, when he came to visit with his wife. They came to discuss what to do with the money from my grandmother's estate. My dad had been waiting years for his share and my uncle had come to explain why he would never get it.

I peek around the doorway just as Johnny says, "Brought you a few things. Be back in a minute." He disappears, then returns a few minutes later with two huge bags. "For you and the little ones."

"What is all this?"

"Open 'em up and see."

My mom pulls out enormous cans of apple juice and spaghetti sauce, giant tins of baked beans, mixed carrots and corn. Uncle Johnny leaves and comes back with more bags, this time loaded with bathroom stuff like toilet paper and tissue boxes. A flat cardboard tray holds enough juice boxes to keep our whole building from going thirsty for a month.

"Johnny, what's going on? What is all this?" asks my mom.

"Well, Sam, it's, you know . . . supplies."

"Supplies for what? A nuclear war?"

"No, for, you know, you and the little ones."

"Johnny, they aren't so little anymore and . . . why now? I don't get it."

Uncle Johnny starts to cry, catching his tears in his big hand, which seems silly because we now have enough tissue to wipe up a tsunami.

My mom leads him to the sofa, stepping over boxes and around cans. "Sit down, Johnny," she says. "I don't understand." She grabs a wad of tissue and gives it to him. He blows his nose, honking like a flock of geese.

"I wasn't here for him. I should've been. I know it now. I wasn't here for him or for you. Christ, Sam, I didn't even come to the funeral. My own little brother. What does that make me?"

I hold my breath behind them because I remember how angry my mom was when he called to say he couldn't come.

"It makes you a turd, Johnny, that's what it makes you.

83

But we forgive you. Really. You don't need to do this, whatever it is you're trying to do. We're all right. Come visit us if you want but don't come in here like you need to rescue us."

They sit for a while, arms around each other, Johnny's crying slowing down. Johnny is built like the army men who came to tell us about my dad, filling up so much space. I wonder what it would be like to live with someone like that. We'd constantly be ducking or pressing ourselves against the wall to let him pass. And those nights when Annie, my mom and I snuggle up together on the couch, my mom in the middle with a bowl of popcorn in the hollow of her crossed legs — where would a man like that fit? He could squeeze into the hard chair across from us but he'd likely break it, like Goldilocks did with the baby bear's chair.

Johnny is still saying sorry, over and over. My mom says it's okay over and over but I can tell she's losing patience. My mom's not the sort of person who likes long displays of emotion. After my dad died, people in the neighbourhood came by with flowers and casseroles for weeks. They'd pat me on the head and pick up Annie. My mom was grateful for the food — it meant she didn't have to cook — but all the sympathy wore her down after a while. Finally, when the doorbell rang, she'd ask me to look through the peephole and, if it was one of the neighbours, to stay really quiet so they'd think we were out. It seemed mean to me but I did it. Eventually they stopped coming.

"Where will you go, Johnny?" Mom finally asks. "Are you going to go home, back to Seattle?"

"I can't, Sam. Not yet. I left such a mess behind me. Such a mess. Things were never the same between us after what I did with, you know, Mom's money. Stacey didn't approve. She was right. I was wrong."

"Did you tell her that? She'll understand if you tell her."

"No, Sam, she threw me out. She's the reason I'm here."

Without another word, my mom gets some spare sheets out of the hall closet and makes up a bed for Johnny on our sofa. "It'll be an early start around here tomorrow. I'm going back to work for the first time in weeks and the girls have school."

"I'll be no bother, you'll see, Sam."

When my mom moves I get a better look at my uncle. His face is covered in whiskers and there are wrinkles around his eyes. I wonder if that's how my dad would look if he were still here. Last time I saw him, on leave six months before he was killed, his skin was tanned because of the hot sun he worked under, but it wasn't that wrinkled.

Then Uncle Johnny turns and sees me. He winks. I don't know what to say so I wave and head to bed.

KRISTA

My mom was shaking me and making me get up. She wanted to change my sheets. She said two weeks was way too long, especially with the way I've been sweating. Whatever. She could change everything around me as long as I was changing too. Sweat was good. It was the weight melting off me.

I had to sit for a while at the edge of the bed until the pounding in my head settled down a little. Then I remembered: my pills. I bent forward, as if getting ready to stand up, and pushed the pills farther in, beyond the hem of the fitted sheet that covered the mattress. Then I made my way to the chair.

She tugged off the old sheets and talked about school, as if I planned to go back. As if changing the sheets would freshen me up and make me ready. She couldn't hear the kids chanting *Crisco, Crisco, Crisco* in my head.

She whipped and flipped on the new sheets, deft and smooth from years of practice at work. No one would have a neater bed than me. You could measure each fold with a ruler and the pleats would be equidistant. Just to make sure, I pulled myself off my chair and offered to help. I took the corner, the magic corner where my pills were, and tucked in the sheet. It was the most exercise I'd had in weeks, apart from going to the hospital.

My poor mom. She thought I really wanted to help. She stood back and watched me with a smile on her face that said, *Glad to see you're feeling better.* As if changing a sheet could erase so much.

When I go back to school tomorrow, I bet I'll find that everyone has fallen apart without me. Tyler says I'm a natural-born leader and he's right. When he dropped me off at home tonight, he pulled a gift bag off the back seat and handed it to me. He said it was to help me go back to school because he knew it wasn't something I really wanted to do. Inside was a brand new cashmere sweater, baby blue and super tight. He made me promise to wear it tomorrow, but he wanted to see how it fit, so I changed in the car. I pulled my old top off slowly, so Tyler could see, even though it was cold. I could feel him looking and resisting the urge to reach over. A note inside the bag said, *To my kitten, purr purr.*

He said he knew it would look awesome on me and it did. I can't wait to put it back on in the morning. The suspension was supposed to punish me and tear me down, but all it did was give me two whole weeks with Tyler, day and night. If that's punishment, I'm ready for more. Every minute with Tyler is so much fun, except when I do something he doesn't like. I waved at someone from the car the other day, someone Tyler had just been talking to, and he grabbed my arm and pulled it down. It hurt but I didn't tell him. I shouldn't have done it. Tyler likes to keep what he does outside the car separate from me and I should know that by now. I won't do that again.

CHAPTER THIRTEEN

In the morning I'm awoken by a scream that makes me leap out of bed and run into the hallway. Annie is standing there, shaking. I run to her and throw my arms around her. She's pointing at the sofa, where our Uncle Johnny's arm is dangling over the back, looking like a loose body part. Annie was asleep when he arrived last night. She has no idea he showed up with bags of gifts. Plus, she's never met our Uncle Johnny.

By now, Uncle Johnny has raised himself up and popped his head over the sofa, scaring her even more. She keeps pointing at Uncle Johnny and saying, "But, but, I thought... You said ..." and that's when it hits me — Annie thinks Uncle Johnny is our father.

Uncle Johnny jumps off the sofa. His hair is sticking out like the bristles of a raggedy broom. He scratches his chin and walks up to Annie, holding out his hand. "Hey there, little one, I'm your Uncle Johnny."

"Oh," says Annie, turning to me.

"It's true," I say. "Dad's brother."

Then Uncle Johnny sticks himself in the bathroom for a long time. We hear the shower running and water splashing at the sink. When he comes out, his hair is washed and combed and he has shaved, so his skin is less shadowy. But Annie, hiding behind me, still won't speak to him. When Johnny walks down the hall toward the kitchen he sees Annie's pictures on the wall. He stops and stares at them for a long time, taking each one in. None of us move. It's like no one is even breathing. Finally, Johnny turns around and looks at us.

"Who drew these? You?" He points at me.

"No, they're Annie's."

"My, my. I can see why I scared you half to death there, little one. You must a thought I'd risen from the dead. Is that right?"

Annie nods.

"So, who'll be needing some lunch around here? I see your Momma's already gone off to work. Who makes the lunches? You?" He points at Annie.

Annie giggles. "No, my sister."

"Oh, your big sister, eh? Well, how 'bout today I make 'em. One thing your Uncle Johnny knows how to do is pack a good lunch. When I work out on the fishing boats, I pack such a great lunch all the guys are jealous. They always think my wife did it, but no, it's always me. She couldn't pack a lunch worth cra .... Anyhow, go get ready. I'm making lunch."

In our room, Annie and I get dressed, pulling our clothes out of over-stuffed drawers. It's weird hearing someone move around in the kitchen when my mom's at work. Usually, I'm the lunch maker. It's my job to move Annie along and get us out of the house on time. When my mother was home with her broken ankle she took over, but her sounds were different than Johnny's — lighter, even on her crutches. It's like Johnny is slamming the sandwich stuff on the counter, pulling open drawers looking for knives or wrap then banging them shut again. When he closes the fridge, it vibrates against the wall. Annie notices too. We keep looking at each other and shrugging.

As I pack my school stuff into my knapsack, I wonder what it would be like if Johnny were my dad. I try to pretend that's him on the other side of the wall, just home from his night watchman job, making lunch for me and Annie. Maybe he'd slip little notes inside with jokes on them. My dad loved knock-knock jokes — the stupider the better. (Him: Knock -knock. Me: Who's there? Him: Arthur. Me: Arthur who? Him: Arthur any more cookies in the jar?) Or he'd write notes, mushy ones that said he loved us or mundane ones reminding us to pick up milk or something on the way home.

I wonder if my mom was thinking like this when she got ready earlier today. She doesn't dwell on the fact that she's alone, at least not in front of us. But when she's alone in her bed, the one she shared with my dad, is it hard for her? Does the space still feel wide and empty without him there or has she gotten used to it?

Now, we hear Uncle Johnny in the living room, folding up the sheets and putting the sofa back together. The air is thick with his trying to be good, to make things right. But when Annie and I are at school, he'll have to look at Annie's pictures all day long and think about what happened to his little brother.

When Johnny hands us our lunches, which are bursting out of their paper bags, he asks if we need him to walk us to school.

"No thanks, Uncle Johnny. We're fine. We've been doing it for years," I say.

My mom would probably love it — she doesn't like that we walk to school alone. It's not that the streets are still dark. It's just sometimes, in the morning, the homeless people haven't gone off to their day spots yet. She says most of them are harmless but she still worries that we'll be scared. We're not. Lots of adults are already out and about and there are other kids walking to school. It's not like Annie and I stick out like targets or anything.

Besides, it's not walking to school that scares me today. It's being there. Chelsea will be back today. Yesterday, her friend Amber was downstairs in the courtyard. She asked me if I'd had any good pizza lately and that's when I knew she knew. It's like she was sending me a warning. But walking up to the school with Uncle Johnny would be like making a dangerous confession, showing my fear. And he can't do anything for me once I'm inside the building.

All I can do is hope that he'll be looking out the apartment window at four, when we trot up the path. Even that would be something.

The sound of my pills shaking in their bottle is soothing. I've been taking the pills for almost two weeks, so I'll have enough for two more. The bottle was supposed to last three months. A warning in red letters states the pills should not be taken in bigger doses or for longer than that, but who's going to know?

Dr. Hatrioff's meal plan is stuck to our fridge. My mom

scurries to make the healthy meals before running off to her preemies. All we have to do is zap them in the microwave. I ate with my dad last night, broiled chicken and steamed carrots, just like in my dream. I had two bites of each. My dad kept chewing and saying, "Yum" but I knew he was craving battered chicken and French fries, food that he could lick off his fingers. I bet after I disappeared into my room he raided the fridge and wolfed down whatever he could find to fill himself up.

When we watched *Jeopardy*, neither of us called out the questions. I kept thinking, *Answer for $500: Wants to disappear. Question: Who is Krista Della Corte?*

CHELSEA

The cashmere felt so rich against my skin. I put an old jean shirt on top so my mom wouldn't see the sweater and ask me where I got it. I'll have to hide it way in the back of the closet so she doesn't find it.

When I'm older, I'm going to arrange everything in my closet by fabric. Tyler's stuff can hang with mine. We'll have a whole row of silk, side by side, his shirts and mine — along with my silk dresses. We'll have another one for leather, our boots lined up against the wall in special holders, a row of jackets in every colour hanging above them. We'll even have a wall for denim. And special drawers for wool, including cashmere. This sweater will be the first of my new collection and I'll keep it forever, even when it's full of holes.

We won't have anything synthetic in our closet. Tyler said that anything worthwhile has to begin with the very best

ingredients. You can't make something special out of crap —
you have to begin with the very finest raw material. He said it's
the same principle for everything: food, clothes, people. Then
he looked at me with those dark eyes of his and said that's
what I had. Perfect raw ingredients. I didn't need additives.
I wondered if he was trying to tell me that I was wearing too
much makeup, so when he was out making a delivery I wiped
some off on my sleeve.

I stood in front of my mirror forever this morning, getting ready to go back to school. I wanted to have the right look,
to give the right message. I didn't want anyone to think I was
scared. I wanted my face to be calm and cool and collected,
with a sly smile, like I was keeping in the world's biggest secret.
Like I knew nothing could hurt me. Not even seeing Tessa
again. I know she didn't tell about what happened outside the
pizzeria. If she did, I'd have heard. I've seen her at Amber's,
always holding her little sister's hand. Once they were even
skipping, like they didn't know how stupid they looked. And
I've seen her with her mom, too. They always hold the little
sister's hands between them. It's so sucky it makes me want
to spit.

CHAPTER FOURTEEN

Chelsea is back at school today, taller and blonder and prettier than ever, blue shadow on her lids and peachy-pink lipstick on her mouth. She's wearing a tight blue sweater that hugs every square inch of her perfect shape. She laughs big and loud down the hallway, like she doesn't have a care in the world and has been off in Disneyland for two weeks.

We have two classes together in the morning, French and English. I can feel her behind me, so I barely hear a word my teachers say. At lunch I sit with my back to her, but Paul tells me that she's watching me the whole time. He can see her chewing and staring, whispering to her friends, then glaring at me some more.

"What's up with her anyway? Why does she care so much about you?" he asks, stuttering the way he does.

"I fought with her . . . because she did something rotten to my friend."

"Oh yeah, what?"

"Didn't you hear about it? She Photoshopped a picture

and taped it to her locker."

"That's all?" Paul's eyes drift far away, like he's reliving some of the stuff that's been done to him at school. I wonder if I should give him more detail, like how it devastated Krista. I decide to let it go but plan to tell Krista that not everyone in the school knows. That will encourage her to come back.

Uncle Johnny has packed enough food for ten people. It's the type of lunch fishermen would need if they'd been out doing hard labour on the sea all morning, hauling in lobster traps or fighting with whales, and it's way too much for me. I spread the food around on the table. Paul and the others help themselves to carrots, cheese, pickles, and extra ham sandwiches. It's like a birthday party.

At one point I work up the nerve to turn around and peek. Chelsea's gang is back together. Now I know it was her absence and not some official ban that was keeping them apart. They're sitting so close, their heads are touching, turning them into a tepee. I imagine them talking about how they want their pound of flesh, like Shylock in *The Merchant of Venice*. I'm glad Krista wasn't in English class this morning —she might have felt the class was looking at her every time Ms. Bane said the word "pound." After class, I heard Chelsea say that Krista could give up a hundred pounds and still have a lot left over. Her friends all cracked up. I stopped dead in my tracks. Not because of what Chelsea said, but because it was the first time I'd heard Krista's name mentioned since I came back to school last week. Even Ms. Bane, our favourite teacher, hasn't asked me about Krista. It's like everyone but Chelsea has forgotten her.

After lunch we have gym. Thank god we're just watching a movie today because our teacher is sick. I'd have been a sitting duck out there on the floor playing basketball or volley-ball or whatever. But Chelsea keeps her distance. She doesn't come up to me in that class or anywhere else. She just lets me know she's there by talking loudly or standing close enough for me to see her. Every time she does it I think how unfair it is that all she got was a two-week suspension for ruining Krista's life.

For the rest of the week, I watch Chelsea take her place back at centre stage. She keeps her distance from me, though, which is good news. I feel myself relaxing more and more each day. At first, I was sitting with my shoulders scrunched up so tightly, it was like they were made of rock. By Friday, I'm leaning back and I only remember Chelsea when she calls out something stupid. Or when I look beside me and see Krista's empty desk.

During history, last period of the week, the speaker in our room crackles on. I'm barely listening but the teacher starts poking my shoulder and I realize it's my name that's blaring over the box. Not just mine. Chelsea's, too. My heart leaps into my mouth. We are both being called into the prin-cipal's office. Just the thought of walking down the hallway alone with Chelsea makes my knees shake, so I grab my books and run out ahead of her.

I'm sitting in the same chair as last time, running through all the reasons Mr. Steinbrenner might want to see us together, when Chelsea saunters in and plunks herself down in the other chair.

"Well, girls," Mr. Steinbrenner begins. He is leaning for-ward, elbows on the desk and palms together as if he's about to start clapping. "I thought we needed to have this little talk to make sure everything is okay between you two now."

"Don't worry, Mr. S.," says Chelsea. "We're in total

harmony, like besties." She turns her head to me and plasters a huge smile on her face.

"No sarcasm, please, Chelsea. I'm serious. I hope that your suspensions gave you ample time to think about how you want to project yourselves as young women in the world. Tessa?"

He stares right at me, so I nod. I'm thinking this would be the perfect time to tell him how Chelsea projected herself at me, along with her sleazy boyfriend. But I can feel Chelsea glaring at me, almost daring me to.

"And I hope you had the opportunity to discuss what you did with someone at home, someone you look up to, maybe your moms. I'm sure they didn't approve of what you did. Tessa, I know your mom didn't when she was here. Chelsea, your mom didn't sound too pleased on the phone. I know neither of you have a dad you can talk to but I am sure your moms are understanding people."

Neither of us responds. I know my mom didn't like the thought of me rolling around on the floor tearing out Chelsea's hair, but if she could see how badly all this has affected Krista, she'd be on my side. Chelsea is suddenly breathing loudly beside me, like she wants to burst. I didn't know she doesn't have a father either.

"My mom doesn't give a — "

"Chelsea, I'm sure that's not true. It might just seem that way."

"No, it *is* that way. Can we go now? I promise to be good." Chelsea holds up her right hand with two fingers splayed out in a peace sign.

"You can both go, but I don't want any more trouble. You need to put the incident behind you and be more careful about the choices you make. If there is another episode, the consequences will be way more serious."

I should scream Krista's name out loud, to bring her into the meeting, but Mr. Steinbrenner is already shuffling papers, moving on to other business. Chelsea is standing at the door. She seems to be waiting for me. I can't sit in this chair forever so I get up. We step through the door together and Chelsea reaches over and pinches me, hard, on the arm. I feel the twist, deep inside my muscle. Then she says, in a really loud voice, "You know I'm sorry, Tessa. I hope we can be friends now?" She smiles that bright smile again and the school secretary looks over at us and smiles too.

Chelsea takes off and I follow. Her hard footsteps echo against the lockers. I walk slowly and quietly behind her, praying she won't turn around. When the bell rings, doors open and kids flood the halls and I lose sight of Chelsea. I grab my books from my locker to get out of here as fast as possible, relieved that it's the weekend and I won't have to see or hear her for two whole days. I'll only have to feel the pinch and watch another bruise sprout, then fade, like the last ones.

Outside, I pull my jacket tight against the chill. The greasy X doesn't show anymore, not unless you hold the jacket up to the light and really look for it. But I can feel it there, on my chest, turning me into a huge target. I walk with my head low, to fight off the fall wind. Light, but cold, rain is falling, creating puddles in the pavement.

Chelsea and her friends are standing at the corner, their arms folded across their chests. I suck in my breath when I realize that I'll have to walk right past them to get Annie. If I pull my hat down low enough, maybe they won't know it's me.

My heart pounds as I walk. I try to use its beat to guide

my feet, one step per beat, as though I'm choreographing a dance. In my head I count, *one two, one two*, breathing in and out deliberately. There are at least five girls in the group, each one a Chelsea clone. I feel an immense pressure between my legs, as if I'm going to pee. That's all Chelsea needs to finish me off for good, so I squeeze my muscles tight, making the contractions part of the dance.

Every muscle in my body tenses as I prepare to be grabbed. But nothing happens. They don't make any moves toward me; they just let me pass. They're dead silent, too. I feel my entire body relax as I run across the street, putting more distance between us. Maybe Mr. Steinbrenner's warning sunk in, even though Chelsea seemed to shrug it off.

Annie comes running out of the building like she always does, her raincoat unzipped, pigtails a mess, knapsack sagging down her back. She throws her arms around my waist and I feel the squeeze way down inside. I zip her up, settle her knapsack on her shoulders, take her hand, and turn toward home.

It's only then that I realize we've been followed.

Before I can think, Chelsea and two other girls grab Annie and pull her away from me. Two others hold me back. No matter how much I kick and scream they won't loosen their grip. I kick so furiously, but I can't get any traction.

Chelsea and the other two carry Annie up the street, away from me. It's like they're tearing away a part of my own body. With each step they take, fear boils through my veins like lava. I fight to get away but they keep yanking me back against the wall. I try to bite and can't reach their skin; their hair hangs loose but I can't grab it. Finally, I manage to twist around so that I can at least see what's going on. Annie's pink raincoat stands out like cotton candy amidst the black and the sight is like a steel cable that hooks into my heart and tugs. But I can't see what Chelsea and her group are doing or hear what they're saying. I hold my breath, praying they'll release her now that they've done what I'm sure they wanted — scare me half to death. At one point I realize I really have peed. The pee is already half frozen, crusting my jeans, turning me numb between my legs. Thank god no one seems to notice — but what does it matter? I'll pee a giant puddle in public if only they'll let her go.

I've done a lousy job protecting Annie: first with the way I handled our father's death and now this. What if this day changes Annie the way that day two weeks ago changed Krista? Still straining against my captors, I think of what I've done for her since. I fought Chelsea once, that's it. And then I let Krista become nothing more than a faded outline of tape on her locker.

Watching Chelsea and her friends push Annie back and forth, like a perverted game of "London Bridge", I vow to do more.

Then suddenly Annie's knapsack flies down the street, unzipped, so that all her pencils and books roll into a puddle. Chelsea picks up a fat marker and spins Annie around. She reaches out and dabs the marker against Annie's face. Annie is squirming, trying not to give her any space to write on. Then Chelsea reaches out and pulls off Annie's pink raincoat. The other two release her for a second so they can pull off the sleeves. When Chelsea has Annie's coat bunched in her arms, she flicks her head. It's the slightest flick, more like she's shaking hair out of her eyes, but her friends catch the signal, even through the rain, and let me go. At the same time, her other friends release Annie.

Annie runs to me, squashing her school stuff even deeper into the water. I bend down and catch her in my arms. She's shaking, wet with tears and rain. I take off my jacket and throw it around her, Then I scoop up as many of her markers and books as I can and shove them into her knapsack. I squish her knapsack inside my own and throw it on my back. Then I fling Annie over my shoulder and take off for home.

The kids are calling me. I hear them across the school yard, yelling at me to come over, like we're playing a game of Red Rover. Red Rover, Red Rover, let . . . don't recognize the name, so I stop running. I stop and I'm nowhere, not back on my side with Tessa and not over on theirs. I'm like a soldier caught in no man's land, totally open and vulnerable to the bullets that might rain down.

Tessa is tugging my arm, pulling me back, back into our safe little corner. But sometimes I get tired of just playing with Tessa. The other kids seem to want me. They're waving at me, flapping their hands so eagerly. They're saying my name, chanting it like a song, encouraging me across the big puddle: Krista, Krista, Krista. *So I shake Tessa off and run, splashing through the water that wets my jeans above my rubber boots. Now that I'm closer I hear them more clearly. I see their mouths wide open, cheering me on like my own private fan club. They should have shiny pompoms in their hands. Their voices hit me loud and clear:* Crisco, Crisco, Crisco. *Can we fry our food in you? I freeze and stand there, wet from the puddle and something else. The wetness seeps down my legs, burning. I stand there, burning, marooned in the Pacific Ocean.*

CHELSEA

I didn't plan what happened after school today. Maybe it was the way Mr. Steinbrenner forced me to say things I didn't mean, like how sorry I was or how I was sure I'd changed in my two weeks at home. When the secretary called our names over the intercom, I thought Tessa had squealed about what happened at the pizzeria. As I was walking to the office, I told myself I didn't care. If I got suspended again I could spend more time with Tyler. I missed him already. When Mr. Steinbrenner asked whether my two weeks at home had made me think about my choices in life, I told him they had, because it's true. I did think about my choices. My best choice was Tyler.

I could see Tessa walking up the street toward her sister's school like she does every day. I knew that in a few minutes they'd come back down together, holding hands like they didn't have a care in the world. Across from the elementary school, my friends and I watched Tessa's little sister run to her and wrap her arms around her waist. The way Tessa hugged her sister and then zipped up her coat — it was like she was her mother or something.

That's when something in me snapped.

CHAPTER FIFTEEN

My mom and Johnny are sitting on the sofa with mugs in their hands, laughing about something, when Annie and I walk in. Johnny must have been telling a story because his hands are up in the air and we can hear his voice booming loudly even as we walk down the hall. My mom is cracking up, laughing in a way I haven't heard for a long time, like she can't stop. Her tea is slopping over the brim of the mug and running down her hand but she just wipes it on her jeans and keeps laughing.

"Hey kids. How was school?" my mom calls out, rising and turning toward us. She stops when she sees Annie's face. "What the — "

"She's okay, Mom," I say, but then Annie starts crying. Johnny gets up too and joins us in the hallway. I don't want anyone breathing me in, I smell so bad.

"Hey there, little Picasso, what happened?" Johnny bends down and scoops Annie up effortlessly.

"Annie? Tessa?" my mom asks, looking for an answer. All I can do is stare at her T-shirt, which is dotted with food stains from the café. I distract myself by trying to figure out what each blob is. But my mom starts shaking my arm, which is still numb from carrying Annie

"Why is Annie wearing your jacket? Tessa?"

"Okay, Mom, okay. It was her, the girl who got Krista. The one that put up that picture. The one I fought with."

"Is this something I should know about, Sam?" Uncle Johnny is back on the sofa, Annie on his lap, but he's so big it's like his face is still there, in the middle of everything. My mom ignores his question.

"Tessa, tell me everything. My god, your arms are frozen." She pulls me into the living room but I can't sit down.

"I'll be right back, Mom." I run to the bathroom and peel the jeans from my legs. I roll them into a tight ball and squash them down at the bottom of the hamper. I'll have to do laundry tonight or these will stink. I wash quickly, then throw on my pyjama pants and a hoodie and go back to where my mom and Uncle Johnny are waiting for an explanation.

I have to tell them everything. My mom paces back and forth the whole time. She keeps picking up the phone and saying that she's calling the cops. Uncle Johnny calms her down and tells her to wait until I'm done. He even winks at me once or twice behind her back.

"Okay, Tessa. Police, no. But a visit to the school, definitely. That's my final offer. This time. But if anything else happens, I am going to the police, no arguments."

After dinner, I shove my wet jeans and a pile of dark clothes into the washer. I sit on the old cracked chair in the basement laundry room and follow spiders as they crawl into cracks in the walls as I think about Chelsea. Maybe I should have let my mom call the police. What if doing something to me, Krista, and now Annie, wasn't enough for her? It strikes me that the attacks were all kind of similar. It's like she wanted to change the way we looked, Krista through the picture, Annie by drawing on her and stealing her raincoat, me by marking up my jacket. She stopped short of scratching my face, but only because her boyfriend signalled that time was up. If he hadn't, I wonder what she would have done.

Back upstairs, I string the load of wet clothes over the clothes horse in the bathtub. My jeans will take forever to dry. I'll move the clothes horse into the living room in the morning, close to the radiator. I can't do that now because of Johnny. If he flings out an arm while he's sleeping he'll knock it over.

When I look around, I notice Johnny isn't there. I ask my mom where he is and she says that he went out earlier, quite suddenly, but she doesn't know where. "All he said was to stay put. As if we would jump into a car we don't own and take off on a family vacation," she adds.

Half an hour later, Johnny walks through the door with Annie's coat over his arm. My mom and Annie and I look at each other. We don't know what to say. I wonder if Johnny has special powers, like the ability to sniff like a bloodhound and follow Annie's scent. Or clairvoyance — where he can feel the presence of some unseen object and locate it. It's like every-thing he does is big, like his lunches. I guess someone like Johnny doesn't know how to do things small. He's probably done everything big all his life, except care about his younger brother. He'd been small about that.

"But how did you find it?" my mom finally asks, as Annie runs to Uncle Johnny.

"I saw that girl — she was down below in the courtyard

and had Annie's coat over her arm. She laid it on the fountain right under the window, almost like she wanted us to see it."

We are all slack-jawed, listening. I'm sure he must be talking about Amber. After all, she was there with Chelsea and she knows exactly where we live. She probably dropped it off on her way home from Chelsea's. I bet she was hiding out until dark.

"And you just happened to see that?" asks my mom. "That's incredible."

"It was pretty lucky I was looking out the window just then," Uncle Johnny admits. "So then I ran downstairs and followed her."

"You what?" I ask. How could he follow Amber? She just lives next door.

"I followed her, all around the neighbourhood, to find out where she lives."

Then it dawns on me — Johnny must be talking about *Chelsea.*

"She turned into an apartment building a few blocks away. I waited a few minutes to make sure she didn't come back out. I knew it was hers by the way she strode up to it and by the way she kicked the door open. You wouldn't do that at someone else's place."

Why would Chelsea take Annie's coat only to return it later? I wish I had seen her face as she laid it over the rim of the fountain. Did she look sorry? Or did she do it just because she knew my mom would want to call the cops?

The smile that spreads across Annie's face when she holds up her coat is enormous. It's the smile I wish I could have given her.

KRISTA

Last night, my chest pain woke me up again. I slid open my window and gulped some cold air, but every time I breathed deeper, the knife came back, jabbing between my ribs.

The moon hung above me, big and round, like a potato chip in the sky. I am like the moon, changing my shape, going from round to thin. Without the pills, I'd keep growing, getting bigger and bigger until I exploded.

I'd become the girl on my locker, a real Goodyear blimp. *Crisco.* One hundred percent fat and nothing else.

CHELSEA

The kid was light as a feather between our arms and her eyes were wide with fear as we pushed her around. Her raincoat was pink like bubble gum, with a hood decorated in yellow and blue umbrellas, the kind of coat I'd always wanted my mom to buy me when I was a kid. All of a sudden, I wanted to get it off of her so badly. It was like if I could get the coat, something would change, but I didn't know what. After it was all over, I walked home with the stupid pink coat rolled under my arm and I couldn't figure out what I was going to do with it. If my mom found it she'd want to know where I got it. I thought of slashing it, but didn't. I don't know what stopped me. I kind of had no choice but to do what I did. I did it on the way out to meet Tyler. I just hope Amber didn't see me.

CHAPTER SIXTEEN

On Monday, Uncle Johnny insists on walking me and Annie to school.

"Come on, girls. Your old uncle needs the exercise. My muscles are turning to jelly, see?" He takes his big fist and pounds his thighs under his jeans, but nothing jiggles. Annie laughs.

"Can he, Tessa?" she asks.

I find it hard not giving in to Annie, especially now, but something in me keeps saying that I have to get us there on my own. Maybe it's like people who've been thrown from horses. They have to get back in the saddle right away or they'll never ride again.

"Not today, sweetie."

I hold Annie's hand tightly as we make our way out of the courtyard. I keep an eye out for Amber. It's funny, but I've lived beside her for so many years and we've never said two words to each other. It's like we don't exist for each other except when Chelsea is around.

I have an awful feeling Uncle Johnny is following us. I keep turning, thinking I'll see him hiding behind an opened newspaper and leaning back nonchalantly against a tree, like in old movies. All around us, leaves are falling off trees, shaken down by wind and rain. Annie stoops to collect a bouquet of red maple leaves and yellow oak leaves. I don't tell her not to, even though I know how dirty they get once they hit the ground. We march up the stairs of her school and into the office where I ask to speak to the principal. I tell her that Annie was roughed up by some older kids so she might be moody today. I also ask her to let Annie sit and wait for me in the office after school, rather than out front, which she says is no problem. When she says she'll have to file a report on the incident, especially if physical violence was involved, I assure her that my mom is doing that up at my school because we know who did it. That seems to make her happy, even though it may not be true. So far, my mom hasn't mentioned reporting Chelsea again and I'm glad. It'll only make everything worse. I want to handle Chelsea myself.

I walk to school, thinking of my other mission — helping to restore Krista to our school. I can't stop thinking about the way nobody at school talks about her. Something Annie's principal said has stuck with me: *We take bullying very seriously here and want all parties involved to be held accountable.* All parties. In Krista's case, there were so many — not just the ones that did it and are easy to identify, but the others, who stood by and laughed. Who have now dismissed the whole thing from their minds, as though she doesn't matter.

I hate to admit it, but I know Annie matters more because she's small and pretty. Bullying her was like crushing a butterfly, but bullying Krista was different. Most people probably think the school looks better without her.

We finish *The Merchant of Venice* in class and learn that Shylock is no monster. He's just a human being who has been subjected to so much prejudice it turned him hard and bitter. When we read his speech about how he still bleeds when cut, like anyone else, Ms. Bane says we should think about that.

"All human beings, no matter what their religion or skin colour, are made of the same biological material," she says. "Therefore, we should all be treated the same way and be held to the same moral standards. No exceptions, so long as we don't break the law."

I turn around and shoot Chelsea my fiercest glance. She's draped over her desk, buried under her hair that covers her like a veil. I can't tell if she noticed me or not. When the bell rings she bounces up, like she's attached to strings.

Walking out of class, I don't say goodbye to Ms. Bane even when she smiles at me. I don't want to be her friend. She said "the" law, like there is only one law to follow. But there are many laws and the hardest ones are not written down. They are just out there, in the air. Everyone knows what they are and tries to follow them, even though no one really knows where they came from. Krista broke one by being fat, my new friend Paul by stuttering. I want to ask Ms. Bane why everyone acts like that's fair when it isn't. Why everyone at school seems to think that Chelsea's two-week suspension was enough when Krista hasn't even been able to come back to school because of what she did. I want to ask Ms. Bane why even she, Krista's favourite teacher, has not mentioned Krista once since I've been back at school.

After school, I take Annie home, then continue on to Krista's. I have to see her to make sure she's all right. The first thing I notice is her skin. Krista used to have creamy skin, without a blemish, but today her face is gray and blotchy. Her normally shiny and bouncy hair is even more limp and stringy, like all the life has been sucked out of it.

"Krista?" I say. She barely unfurls herself from the tight ball she is coiled in.

"What do you want?" she says, wincing as she shifts.

"What's wrong?"

"Stomach ache. That's all. What do you want?"

I want to tell her that I want her to stop taking those pills. To be who she used to be. But I can't find the words. "Go away, Tessa," she says. She holds her middle and moans, like she's riding the wave of a bad cramp. "Please, just go away."

I look at the mattress where the pills had been. There's no way I'm going to be able to check if they're still there now. Every time Krista talks I can see the pain on her face. I'm only making her worse.

So I leave. But I know I've got to do something for her. And fast.

When I add my own story to the Web, I'll need a new name. Maybe something like Crystal, or Crystal Light, like the drink, which is what I'll be by then. I'll say how losing weight changed my life, like it changed for all those other girls online. Maybe other fat girls will read my story and be inspired by it. They'll pass my name around from person to person. I might even work up the nerve to post a picture of the new me.

I wish Tessa wouldn't come over until I'm finished

changing. Right now, I've only lost fifteen pounds. I want to make it twenty. When that happens, I'll bounce out of bed, wash my hair, and make it curly and shiny again. It'll fall even more elegantly over my shoulders and down onto my new, slimmer chest. I'll walk with a real bounce in my step and make my hair bounce with me. If I do go back, kids at school won't recognize me. They'll think I'm a new kid. Maybe I could really change my name to Crystal and be someone new. Cancel out the old me altogether, like she never really existed.

CHELSEA

Tyler loves the way I don't talk too much when I'm with him. He said some girls don't know when to keep quiet. He said it's an art, knowing things like that just by instinct and not because anyone taught you. That's another reason he quit school. He wasn't learning anything useful there. And I'm not either. It all seems so pointless, the teachers going blah blah blah about all kinds of things that I don't care about now and probably never will.

Besides, lots of famous people never finished high school, like Britney Spears and Kelly Osbourne. And it didn't hurt them at all. It probably just gave them more time to work on becoming the people they are now. Tyler said I shouldn't quit. I don't know why he'd say that to me. He said I should wait until I have something sure to go to, like his plan with the pizzerias, or the modelling. But that could take a long time. I want to start working on myself now, before I'm too old.

Besides, I have a feeling I'll be kicked out soon anyway because of what happened with Tessa's sister. I keep waiting for my name to crackle over the loudspeaker again, summoning me back to the office. Maybe that's why I did it. Maybe I want out of here so badly, I screwed up again. If that does happen, my mom will kill me. And Tyler? He tells me to stay in school but that he misses me in his car. Right now, I'm just confused.

CHAPTER SEVENTEEN

On Friday after dinner Uncle Johnny stretches his legs and says, "I'm going for a walk, kid. Come on with me." He throws me my jacket and holds the door open. I look at my mom but she just shrugs. Annie will have to help her with the dishes tonight. Johnny cooked a whole tub of homemade spaghetti sauce loaded with zucchini and mushrooms. We'll have enough left over in the freezer for a month.

"Where are we going?" I have to walk fast to keep up with Johnny's long legs, taking two steps for every one of his.

"There are things that need sorting out in this family, Tessa. Lots of things. I can't just go off with this mess hanging over you. No siree. If Jake were here, he'd be doing the same. I owe him, kid. I owe him."

I seriously hope Johnny isn't going to cry. I used to hate it when my dad cried. When I thought of him crawling through sand on his belly or combing the rubble, it was such a tough image. But when he cried it softened him up and I had trouble putting the two pictures together.

"But where are we going?"

"We're going to find that girl and have it out. She needs to know she can't keep threatening you and Annie and get away with it. It's the least I can do — sort out that mess before I go home."

Johnny's going home? He seems so settled with us all of a sudden. My mom loves knowing he's there to see us off to school and help with dinner. I haven't seen her so happy in years and it isn't just because she's back at work.

"I really don't think that's a good idea. I don't want to talk to her. I've never talked to her. You don't talk to girls like her." I stop walking and wait for him to stop too, but he doesn't.

"Don't you know your Uncle Johnny is the mediator? Out on the boats, big guys get into fights over stupid things all the time. We'll be gone for weeks and it's rough being in such a tight space. I've seen guys want to kill each other for stepping one inch too far into someone else's quarters. Who always gets them to calm down and sort things out? Me. You might say I missed my calling."

"Calling?"

"Yeah. I could've been a counsellor or a priest. A go-between of some kind. Only one person I was never able to smooth things out with and that was your father, my little brother. We were always like bulls, locking horns over everything."

Johnny picks up the pace, like the memory of my dad is driving him even harder, until I'm practically jogging. Suddenly he stops, plants his feet apart and points to a building that looks a lot like my own, only without the fountain. *Now what?* I think. Is he going to stand in the yard and yell Chelsea's name until she floats onto the tiny iron balcony, like

Juliet? Is he going to throw stones at every window until her blond head appears, flashing against the dark sky like a beacon? Is there any way I can talk him out of this? The thought of standing inches away from Chelsea and having a conversation horrifies me. Johnny's acting as if you can reason with a girl like her, just point out through words that was she's doing is wrong. Like she's simply stepping over a little line. But he's wrong. It's her whole way of seeing girls like me and Krista that needs changing, and no conversation is going to do that.

We cross the street and squeeze between two parked cars. Lots of noise is coming from behind the building, where a long driveway leads to an underground garage. Doors are slamming and angry voices carry on the night air over the beat of bass from car speakers. I think this might make Johnny turn away but it doesn't. We start along a pathway to the front door. It's dark because only one street lamp is lit. This is exactly the type of scenario my mom always warns us away from. Has Johnny lived on the sea for so long that he doesn't recognize dangers on dry land? Does he only know waves and sharks and hurricanes? My mom told me he has fished in Asia and the Mediterranean. I wonder if those waters hold other dangers, maybe even pirates. My heart is pounding. My only consolation is Johnny's size. I am completely hidden by his body. In a pinch, he could pick me up and throw me over his shoulder, like I did with Annie, only easier.

Johnny pulls open the front door and we step into the lobby. Mailboxes line one wall, a round white buzzer on top of each. Only a handful of boxes have name tags in the slots. Most people have decided to remain anonymous, including Chelsea. Johnny scans the boxes, scratching his chin. He looks down at me and shrugs, like it just occurred to him that this might not be as easy as he thought. The disappointment is heavy in his eyes. I know he was picturing us walking into Chelsea's apartment, sitting down, and having a civilized conversation with her and her family. He'd be in the middle, pacing around, practising his skills as a mediator, fixing everything. Then he could go back to Oregon or out on the next fishing vessel without worrying about us.

"Let's go home, Uncle Johnny," I say. "It's okay, we tried."

Johnny doesn't say no. He lets me lead him outside. The noises around the corner have grown even louder, with more car stereos competing for air space. I want to be home. Chelsea's building is only blocks from my own but I feel like I'm in a completely different neighbourhood, maybe because I rarely go out at night.

Johnny's looking back, scanning the rows of lit windows like he's still hoping to see Chelsea. We're at the end of the path when we hear a hard thud against the brick. A male voice cuts the air, yelling at someone to get back in the car. Johnny pushes me gently behind the one and only tree and turns back up the walkway. I'm straining to hear, but I can only catch a few phrases, like "I told you" and "better listen." A softer voice answers back with "Sorry." It's muted, like it's hard for the girl to speak. I run and crouch behind a bush that gives me a clear view of the side wall.

A guy is holding a girl against the brick, his hands on her arms, pinning her there. He leans toward her and talks into her ear. He's too far away for me to hear but whatever he's saying is making the girl nod. Her hair flops over her shoulders, like she's shaking. Just then, a car turns into the driveway. The man steps aside and the car's headlights illuminate the girl's face long enough for me to see it's Chelsea and that she's

117

crying. Her face is so different from the way it is at school, perfectly arranged and composed. Now, her features look melted and badly put together, her makeup smeary.

I watch in horror as Johnny strides up to the man and yanks him back. I see his face and freeze. The guy from the pizzeria. I want to tell Johnny we should run but I don't want to draw attention to myself. The pizza guy is smiling, like he finds it all funny. It's the same smile that crossed his face the day he asked if I was "her," then bruised my arms. So many times since that day I have thought that if he ever touched me like that again I'd die, it was so creepy.

And here he is, doing the same thing to Chelsea.

"You okay, young lady?"

"Get lost, old man," the pizza guy says. "She doesn't need your help. She's with me."

"Yes, and I think being with you is the problem. That's no way to treat a girl."

"Who the hell asked you for advice?"

Johnny ignores him and asks Chelsea if she's alright again.

"Ah, screw this. I'm outta here. But you think about what I said." The guy wags his finger in Chelsea's face one last time while she cringes. Then he walks to his car, the one with the giant pizza on top. Why didn't I see it before? If I had, I would've run away without looking back.

Uncle Johnny is still with Chelsea. "Is there anyone I can call for you, young lady?" he asks. "Your parents? Can I go get someone to come for you?" He places his hand gently on Chelsea's shoulder, like he's ready to lead her home. I watch as Chelsea recomposes her face. It's like watching a jigsaw puzzle rearrange itself into perfect interlocking order.

"Leave me alone, you old pervert. Who the hell are you, anyway? This is none of your business," she says, shrugging off Johnny's hand.

"I'm just an old guy who cares. So, I'll ask again — is there anyone I can go get for you, to help you home?"

"No, there's no one. You get it? So leave me the hell alone."

Chelsea marches around the corner toward the door. I think it's now safe to pop up from behind the bush. I need to lead Uncle Johnny away before the pizza guy returns. But I pop up too soon. Chelsea looks back over her shoulder and our eyes lock. The two of us freeze, staring at each other over the dim courtyard. Johnny stands between us, tall as a tree.

Chelsea glares at me hard, but in a different way than usual. Like she is trying to figure me out, not like she wants to kill me. Then she turns and disappears. Thank god, Johnny doesn't try to follow her.

KRISTA

My world has become so small. It's me in my white bed under the window. When the sun shines through, it spreads green from my curtains onto my white bedspread like new grass. It's my parents' footsteps coming and going, sometimes with food. It's their hushed whispers talking about how to help me.

They think the world is something I can step back into. They don't know that the world has floated far, far away. It would take me days just to touch it with my toes.

They try to fill me up with words about how pretty I am

and how smart I am, but everything they say grates on my nerves, like nails on a chalkboard.

Why can't they just leave me alone? I don't need them. I don't need anyone or anything except my trusted pills.

CHELSEA

Wild fires are roaring through Beverly Hills, burning up mansions. They showed pictures on TV. The fire looked like giant orange caterpillars crawling through the mountains, with fountains of ash falling onto roofs. I wonder if the stars could feel the heat from the flames while swimming in their pools. Would they keep swimming even if their houses were burning? I guess people like that don't worry about losing everything. If their house burns down they can just buy another one, maybe even a better one. And they can have all new furniture delivered the next day, just like that.

There is only one thing in the world I'm afraid of losing and that's Tyler. If I lose him, I'll never replace him. I'm such an idiot for not doing what he said. He told me to wait for him in the car. He told me never to spy on him. But when he pulled up to my own building I couldn't help it. I wanted to know what he was doing back there. I could even hear girls' voices behind the building. What if he was fooling around with one of my friends? And why could they be out there when I had to crouch down in the passenger seat like a dirty secret?

All I wanted was a peek. So I got out of the car and followed him. I stayed close to the building, where it's dark. He was leaning against one of the parked cars smoking. I could smell the weed. I heard the other guy say it was good stuff and

Tyler laughed. Girls I didn't know were hanging around, waiting their turn. "Told you," Tyler said. The guy pulled out his wallet and gave Tyler some cash and Tyler handed over a bag.

When Tyler started back toward the car, I didn't move. I wanted to tell him that he didn't need to hide it. I was okay with it. But then he saw me and went crazy. I could feel his spit on my skin. I saw all of my nice new clothes fade away. The modelling jobs too. Someone else's picture would be on top of Tyler's cars, flying through the city. Everything good in my life disappeared, and when his car zoomed away I wanted to scream. Now there really was no one. The old guy didn't believe me. But it was true. There was no one.

Upstairs, I put my ear to my mom's door. There was no sound. I had no idea what she was doing in there. She didn't call out. She didn't ask if I'd had fun or if I was hungry. For all I knew, she was already in a deep sleep. My half-brother's card was open on the kitchen table. She had obviously left it out for me to sign so she could mail it tomorrow. It had a big gold 18 on the front, with "Happy Birthday Son" under it — the whole background floating balloons. Inside was some gushy rhyme about not believing *how time has flown* and *how you have grown*.

The world is full of lies. Only a few things are true. And the truest thing of all, for me, is Tyler.

CHAPTER EIGHTEEN

Saturday night Paul meets me at Karen and Matt's to babysit. I told them we have to work on a school project and it isn't a lie. The kids are shy around Paul until he gets down on the floor and plays horsie, taking turns riding each kid around the dining room table. When they shout "Giddy-up," Paul throws his head back and whinnies like a real horse. Then we play hide-and-seek in teams, Paul and I each taking one kid and crouching behind the sofa or curtains. The kids squeal and squirm, like they can't wait to be found. After two hours of play, they're both exhausted. We put them to bed and take turns reading to them. As I listen, I'm amazed by how Paul's stutter has disappeared. He seems so different here, like he can just let go and be himself.

Then we hit the computer, the real reason for meeting here. Paul knows his stuff. He can scan and cut and paste and enlarge and modify, all things that would take me forever. He moves the mouse from square to square, clicking furiously, like he's done this millions of times before. I try to follow the clicks but soon give up and let him have control. He knows what he's doing and the pictures come out perfectly, just like I saw them in my mind last night. I had no trouble finding the pictures I wanted to use. They were all in a box in my drawer, right beside my bed.

Next, we need to make the signs that will go with them. We work for another hour, experimenting with different fonts and borders. Matt said he didn't mind if we used their printer, so that's what we do. The pictures are coloured but we print the signs in black and white so we won't use all their ink. Besides, the letters stand out more this way.

Matt drives us home around midnight. Paul's house is closest and when he says goodbye he hesitates, like he wants to say more. But Matt's fingers are tapping the steering wheel and that makes us both shy. We plan to meet early Monday morning, before the halls flood with kids.

I'm surprised that my mom is still awake, talking to Johnny. His huge duffel bag sits at the foot of the sofa, looking like it did the day he showed up. When he sees me stare at it he says, "Never stay anywhere more than a few weeks, Tessa. Guests are like fish. They'll start to stink." It will be two weeks tomorrow since Johnny showed up but it seems so much longer. It's weird how you can get used to somebody so fast.

I wonder if Johnny told my mom what he and I saw yesterday at Chelsea's. What would be the point in telling her? It's not like she'll want to help Chelsea, not now. I can still see Chelsea's face when the headlight caught it, the fear in her eyes, and it makes me shiver.

In the morning, Uncle Johnny hugs each of us in turn and says goodbye. Annie cries and so does my mom. Johnny's sniffly too. He tries to joke about how he hopes his "old lady," our Aunt Stacey, will take him back. "Living with you guys made me see what I've been missing most," he says. "Family. Yup, that's the thing. Family. Jake was a lucky man. I'm sure he knew it."

Jake — my dad's name. I'm not used to hearing it. And if my dad was so aware that he had family, why had he spent so little time with us in the last years of his life? But then I see him down on one knee, hugging me and crying. And then my mom, placing a tiny Annie in his arms, how that really set him off. It must have been really hard for him to leave us again. And I remember that picture of him and his friend with the kids in the orphanage, how happy they looked. Maybe his friend had left kids behind too. Maybe those Afghan kids had taken our place in their lives, even just for a few hours.

Like Johnny took *his* place for these past weeks.

Johnny pulls me aside so we can be alone. He bends down on one knee so our faces are level. His skin is deeply lined even though he isn't that old. I guess it's the work he does out on the fishing boats, facing the hot sun and salty wind. But his eyes are friendly behind the crinkly skin, like they're still the eyes of a very young man, full of dreams.

"Tessa," he says. "That girl we saw Friday. That is one unfortunate girl living one unfortunate life." He hangs his head and shakes it slowly. "I'm not saying what she did to you and Annie was right in any way, I'm just saying it takes a whole lot of understanding in this world to know why people do what they do. And you don't have to be a genius to know where that girl's anger is coming from. Whatever else, remember that you have so much more, Tessa. So much more. And she knows it."

Then he hugs me and leaves.

KRISTA

A knife twisted in my gut all night long. If I was back on Dr. Hatrioff's table, would she feel the blade under all my flesh? Last year, we had shots for swine flu at school. As I rolled up my sleeve, I wondered if the needle would be long enough to reach my veins. A kid called across the gym, *Hey Porky, getting vaccinated against yourself?*

This morning, I turned my face to stone when my dad said goodbye. And when my mom asked how I was feeling I said *Okay*, my new favourite word. Ask me anything and I'll say *okay*. I'm like a puppet. Nod, nod, nod. When she started going on about school and how I was ruining my future, I just nodded. *Will you think about it*, she asked me. *Okay, okay.* Nod, nod.

I don't feel bad about lying. People have been lying to me all my life, like my dad calling me his princess and saying I was the prettiest girl on earth. Why would he say that? He knows what pretty is. He watches TV. No one on TV looks like me unless she's playing the ugly girl or she's the "before" on a weight loss show and a skinny person is making her run around a gym. At the end of the show, the fat girl comes out like a whole new person, which is exactly what I'm trying to do. If only it didn't hurt like hell.

CHELSEA

I wish I had a stylist to help me. She could straighten my hair and do my make-up. She could give me that perfect look, layer by layer, the look that could be on the cover of a magazine. On my own, it's hard to tell when that look is ready. I stare into my mirror forever, trying to tell. But every time I think I'm ready, there's always a voice that says I'm not.

I did my best tonight when I went to the pizzeria to find Tyler. When the car pulled up, I combed my hair off my face with my fingers, the way Tyler likes it. It took him a minute to see me. Everything in me froze when our eyes locked. Then he winked and my entire body let go. When he nodded his chin toward the car, my insides floated up like the balloons on my brother's card.

Tyler never said a word about what happened the whole time we were driving. He told me to ring a few doorbells and hand over the tips. I had used my sweetest-smelling shampoo and not even the pizza could cover up the lilacs. When the stack of boxes was gone, Tyler pulled up behind an empty warehouse. I decided I would wait patiently while he did his business. I'd redo my lip gloss, apricot-peach.

The only sound in the car was Tyler, tapping his fingers on the steering wheel. Eventually, another car pulled up. Tyler turned to me and put his finger over his lips, to keep me quiet. I watched him get out and walk over to the car. Seconds later, he motioned for me to come out and join him. He met me halfway and put his arm around my shoulders. My heart was pounding but I kept smiling. When we got to the other car the guy inside said, "This her?" and Tyler nodded. "Nice," the guy said. "Real nice." Maybe this was his friend in the modelling business. If so, I made a good first impression. They did their deal and Tyler handed me the money and told me to keep it safe for him in the car. Then he spun me around and pushed me back. I could feel the two of them watching as I walked, so I swayed my hips a little. Tyler would like that.

When Tyler came back to the car a few minutes later, he leaned over and said "Good job." I thought he'd stroke my thigh again but he didn't. Instead, he kissed me. I could feel his tongue in my mouth, pushing. Then he straightened up and waved at the man, who was driving past in the other car. The man gave Tyler a thumbs-up and smiled. I didn't want to, but I thought of my mother and what she would say. Then I looked at Tyler and I forgot about her. All I thought of were Tyler's eyes, telling me how pretty I looked.

CHAPTER NINETEEN

Paul and I meet early Monday morning, as planned. I have to bring Annie, but that's okay. She's a good helper. Paul brought a big steel tape roller with sharp teeth from home and Annie becomes a pro at taping and tearing. We start at Krista's locker. There, we put up the best picture of her I was able to find. It was taken last summer at the river park, the day she and I biked over with a picnic. She's leaning against a tree, smiling under the sun, her gorgeous hair falling into her lap.

Paul printed up the picture so that it's double its original size, but not as big as the last one that hung there. We want her to look natural. When Annie seals the edges, we can see the old tape scars surrounding it, like a reminder of what we're trying to undo. Underneath we place one of the signs we made on Saturday:

Krista Della Corte
Honours Student at Jackie Robinson Junior High

Winner of the Annual Student Writing Competition
2009 & 2010
Missing from School since September 15th

Underneath that we hang a long sheet of blank paper. Paul writes the first note: *Hey Krista, we miss you.* Annie draws a cloud and in it she writes, *I love you Krista.* We're taking a chance, leaving so much room for messages. We won't be able to control what people write. We just hope that enough of the notes will be positive.

Then we whip around the school, tacking up pictures of Krista on the bulletin boards. We even sneak into the teachers' lounge. I'm especially looking forward to putting this one up. Under the picture the sign reads, *Krista Della Corte: A+ student: Remember me?* I hope the teachers choke on their food when they look up and see it. Outside the gym we hang a picture of Krista holding a volleyball in her raised hands. It was taken at a tournament last year where everyone had to play. Krista didn't want to because she knew no one would want her on their team, but it turned out that she had a mean serve. She helped her team win by firing that first ball so hard over the net that none of the opposing players could touch it. They skinned their knees trying. That sign says: *Krista Della Corte: Ace Server.*

We aren't sure about the cafeteria. Do we want kids looking at Krista while they eat? Will that only make them remember her size? But Paul convinces me it's right. "We want to cover all the places she would be if she were still here, don't we?" he says. And he's right. We do. We want to put her presence back in the school, back into the place that has forgotten her. We decide to hang it right inside the cafeteria, beside the door. This is a more sombre picture of Krista: she isn't smiling or doing anything. She's just staring straight ahead, like she's deep in thought. Under it we hang the sign that says: *Krista Della Corte: Deep Thinker.*

A voice startles us and we jump. So far, we haven't seen a soul. The bell won't ring for another half hour.

"Hey, that's your friend, isn't it?" The cafeteria lady stands staring at the picture, her hands on her hips above her apron.

"Yeah, it is."

"I wondered what'd happened to her. Haven't seen her here for ages." She pokes her finger into her hairnet and scratches, as if that helps her think.

"She's been gone for three weeks now, because of what happened."

"I heard about that. Terrible. Just terrible. Give her my best, will you? Tell her I look forward to having her back here." Then she disappears into the kitchen.

Paul and I just look at each other and smile. The pictures are working. They're jogging people's memories of Krista, making her real and present. I don't know how Krista will feel about what we're doing, given that she's at home trying to make herself invisible, but it feels so right to me.

Finally, I have to leave to take Annie to school. I do it quickly because I don't want to miss a thing. I want to be here when people first notice the pictures, to see their reactions.

All day Paul and I walk around, watching people stop to look at Krista's locker. They stare like they're seeing Krista for the first time or seeing her in a different way. A few people take out pens and scribble notes. I'm dying to peek in the teachers' lounge. At lunch, Paul and I hang out nearby, trying to glimpse inside when someone opens the door. At one point, Ms. Bane steps out. She stops when she sees us and gives us a funny look. We don't shrink. We stare right back.

"Was that your idea, Tessa?" she asks, pointing to Krista's picture. She doesn't sound angry or surprised. Just neutral.

"It was *our* idea." I point beside me, to Paul.

Ms. Bane hesitates, like she can't think what to say. "How is Krista?"

"She's not well. She's really sick. And it's like nobody here gives a damn."

"Tessa, that's not true. I'm sure lots of people are worried about her."

"Yeah, like us. You are looking at the only two people who care. I've been back at school for two weeks now and nobody's asked me a thing. Not even you."

"I don't know what to say, Tessa. Really, I don't. Give her my best, will you?" Then she walks away. She didn't try to deny my accusation. She really hasn't thought about Krista until now.

Mission accomplished.

After school, before running up to get Annie, I stop to read the messages on Krista's locker. A lot of people have written *Get well soon* or *How's it going, Krista?* Some just drew smiley faces. I wonder why there are no nasty messages from Chelsea and her gang and then it hits me: Chelsea is always careful not to leave a record. She likes to do her damage and flee. Even the way she returned Annie's coat suggests that. Maybe that's the only way she can keep dealing with her own life — to pretend that her actions never happened. Maybe if I hadn't fought with her that day in the hall, no one would have known she was responsible for taking Krista's picture. I made her public, in a way. I think of what I now know about Chelsea. I could really hurt her by letting people know that her older boyfriend pushes her around. That would take away her perfect image.

But I won't do it. I remember Uncle Johnny telling me that I have so much more than Chelsea. And it's true. I don't need to bring her down. She does that herself by hanging out with that creep.

I am the little girl in the pink tutu. Watch me twirl. My arms rise above my head in a perfect arch. You are butterflies, not giant turtles. Fly, don't lumber, *the dance teacher says. My pink legs stretch out under me as I leap across the hardwood floor, my eyes on the mirror, amazed at how much I look like the graceful swans that swim at the park my dad takes me to when my mom works late.*

I stand on the edge of the lake and see myself in the water that ripples when the swans swim. The girl in the water is not me. She is someone big who takes up half the lake. She is so big, someone behind her says, She better not fall in, she'll cause a flood.

I am glad I am not that girl. I am glad I am the girl in the tutu, toes pointed, hair pulled up, long neck reaching up to heaven.

I don't care about all those pictures of Krista that are suddenly everywhere. Krista, the girl everyone says I hurt. I don't spend any time thinking about whether it's true or not. She is nothing to me. I didn't even remember her face until I saw it on her locker. When I looked at it it was like I'd never seen her before. The big brown eyes, the long dark curly hair around a heart-shaped face with a nice smile — I couldn't recall any of it. All I remembered was her size.

Everyone at school is writing messages to her about how they hope she'll get better soon. How they miss her. But she makes no difference in my life. So, that's what I wrote. I don't care how it sounds. We aren't connected in any way. I didn't make her fat in the first place, so why is everyone blaming me? I heard that she's losing weight so maybe I did her a favour. She should be thanking me instead of staring out of all these pictures like I've killed her.

Nothing matters now except that Tyler and I are reconnected. If Krista comes back, I'll just leave her alone. It won't matter if she still has all that fat waddling down the hallway. I know how to take care of myself. If I looked like that, I'd never have met Tyler. And if I hadn't met Tyler, I'd be writing something very different right now. So different, I can't even imagine it.

CHAPTER TWENTY

A few days later the doorbell rings out of the blue, after dinner. We all look at one another like we're trying to guess who it might be. My first thought is maybe Uncle Johnny's "old lady" didn't take him back and he's returned to live on our sofa. My mom inhales deeply before looking through the peephole and she hesitates before opening up. From the table, Annie and I see a strange man in the doorway.

"Yes?" my mom asks.

"Are you Mrs. Deane? Samantha Deane?"

"Yes."

"My name is Alex. Alex Davinchuk. I knew your husband, Jake. I was with him in Afghanistan." That final word hangs in the air, freezing us, until my mom finally opens the door wide and signals for him to come in.

"These are my kids, Tessa and Annie. Sit down, please." We gather in the living room, Alex on the chair and the three of us on the sofa.

"I've wanted to come for a long time now, but I wasn't

in good shape. I did rehab for months and then, well, for the next few years . . ."

"It's okay. You don't need to explain. You don't owe us anything."

"No, that's not true. I do. I owe you. I owe him. Your husband saved my life."

"Oh, I see. Well . . . Tessa, put the kettle on please." I want to protest, but I know my mom is stalling for time, getting herself ready to hear what Alex has to say. I hurry to the kitchen, remembering the two men who sat in our living room five years ago to tell us about my father. Their big bodies sank so deeply into our sofa I was sure their bums were hitting the floor. They had taken off their caps and were holding them in their laps, twisting them around as they spoke. The kettle sends a shrill whistle into the air. I pour the water into the pot, put mugs, milk and sugar on a tray, and rush back to the living room. I don't want to miss a word. My mom puts her arm around Annie and pats the other side of the sofa for me. She pours the tea and passes a cup to everyone, including me and Annie, who drowns her tea in sugar.

"Okay, go on, please. Don't worry about the kids. I want them to know everything. They're old enough."

Alex goes on to tell us the most incredible story about the day it happened. He speaks in a soft voice, hanging his head, like he wants to hide in his collar. He's so unlike those other army men, whose voices boomed off the walls. That day, I imagined their grumbles reaching through the slats of Annie's crib and shaking her awake, like a bogeyman. Now, here is Annie, sitting with us to hear Alex fill in the blanks between the crude details that those other men gave us: IED, roadside, eight men, medivac, Germany, surgery. Death.

They were on a routine inspection of a town in southern Afghanistan, near Kandahar. My dad's unit went ahead as usual, to make sure it was safe. They did what was called a cordon and knock, where they go from home to home looking for insurgents. But they found nothing. They knew the town. They had been there before and had spent time at an orphanage, playing with the kids. After searching several homes they had gotten into the truck and were heading back to the base to meet up with other soldiers from the unit. They were whistling. It had been a good day — no insurgents, no insults. They had given candy to the kids, as always.

"The sun was shining," Alex says slowly. "The sky was deep blue. If you looked up, you'd never know there was a war on. We weren't being as careful as we should've been. Me and Jake were sitting in the back, waving at people. We always did that, if we could."

Alex pauses and takes a sip, rattling his cup when he puts it back down.

"After the explosion, we all flew twenty feet into the sand. Flames were bursting all around us. Jake got up first, on his elbows. Somehow, he managed to grab me and drag me away from the flames. My chest had taken the hit." He draws an X over his sweater, showing us where he was wounded.

"You probably know the rest. We were flown to Germany with the third survivor. Everyone else, five men, were killed on the spot, no chance. What saved me and Jake was the fact that we liked to sit in the back and wave at the kids."

By the time he's finished talking, Alex is crying. He takes lots of short deep breaths and I think he's going to faint but then he tells us he suffered lung damage in the explosion and often has difficulty breathing.

We all just sit and say nothing for a long time and it's like that is exactly the right thing to do. To just sit there and let the pictures soak in, even the bad ones. I can hear my mom sniffling beside me. She holds my hand and squeezes tightly and I'm sure she's doing the same with Annie's on the other side. I focus all my thoughts on the picture of my dad smiling under the blue sky in the back of a truck, waving at little kids who were sucking on sweets.

"I have this for you," Alex says. "Jake loved this picture. He had it on him in the hospital. I shouldn't have taken it. It's against the rules 'cause everything goes to the family. I'm sorry. I just wanted it so bad." Tyler hands over the picture my father showed us on his last visit home. There they are: Jake and Alex, sitting on the sand in front of an orphanage, little kids hanging all over them. The picture is creased and faded, as though the smoke rubbed some of it out, but it's still wonderful.

"How did you find us?" I ask.

"I got your address long ago, from Jake. Guys do that, you know. Swap addresses, in case. A friendly face maybe, to tell how it really was. But the longer time went on. . . until I got that call."

"Call?" my mom and I say together.

"From Johnny, Jake's brother. A few days ago. He said you all would want to see me. Until then, I wasn't sure. I mean, it should've been me. If he hadn't come back for me. And I don't have kids. I'm alone." I think he might start crying again, but he doesn't. My mom goes over to him and puts her hand on his shoulder.

"If Jake had just left you there to die, Alex, I wouldn't have wanted him to come back home. Do you get that? What you just told me, that Jake risked his life to save a friend, that is my Jake. You brought my Jake home for me. Thank you." My mom bends down and kisses Alex on the head.

Five years ago, after those army men left, I wandered outside to sit on the edge of the fountain. I was trying to remember being down there with him, in the courtyard. I wanted to remember the way he pushed me on the old rusty swing set, or chased me around to catch and tickle me. But those images were fading already. He'd been gone too long. We'd been alone, just me and my mom and Annie, for three whole years by then. Maybe it wasn't going to make much difference, his being gone, but I wanted it to.

My dad had tried to explain to me that he wanted to help girls like me have more freedom, but in helping those girls he'd missed out on being with me and Annie. I think my dad knew it, because sometimes, when I was telling him about a school concert or fun party, his eyes would get glossy and he'd look far away, maybe like he was back in the desert. Like my words were making him retreat into the rocky caves that I had overheard him describe to my mom.

Alex finishes his tea and tells us how he had to go to rehab for his chest but the rehab led to his addiction to pain killers. Then his fiancée, who had waited for him all through his service years, broke up with him. "That shattered me as bad as the explosion," he says. "And then, I simply got lost. Not really lost, as in I couldn't find myself on a map, but lost inside myself. For many years, I didn't want to live." My mom, who is sitting on the arm of Alex's chair, puts her hand on his shoulder and squeezes.

I wonder if Alex's fiancée tied yellow ribbons around her home to welcome him back. Was she happy to see him at first, until she saw how messed up he was? And how long did it take her to decide she didn't want to be with him anymore, when he couldn't get back to who he was before? The idea of dumping someone because they've changed scares me. I'm sure my mom wouldn't have done that to my dad.

I can't help thinking about Krista. She's taking those pills to lose weight but they're doing way more. They're changing who she is. I see her face as it was the last time I visited, pasty and grey, her stringy hair plastered flat against her pillow. She barely looked at me, like her eyes couldn't focus.

I've got to make sure she knows I'm still here for her.

Nobody is with me in this cocoon. Nobody but me and a million voices in my head. When I close my eyes I hear them. When I fall asleep I hear them, laughing. But they shouldn't be laughing. Not when my stomach is twisting and burning. Not when I'm falling off the balance beam. The beam was in my head. I walked it, toe in front of toe. As I started to wobble my stomach heaved. When I hit the mat my stomach burned, like someone was poking it with a flame. And all around me, bouncing off the high gym walls, was laughter. Laughter poured through the basketball hoops and climbed the ropes and ladders. It ran along the skywalk, dribbling out onto the scoreboard. I tore myself awake to stop it and that's when I knew the burning wasn't a dream. It was real. So real, I covered my middle with a pillow, to make it stop. But it didn't. The burning shot up through the middle, up my neck and into my mouth. I buried my face into the pillow and screamed.

CHELSEA

I wonder if people who become famous remember the exact moment when their lives changed. Like, when they knew that the person they always wanted to be was finally here, in front of them. I had that moment last night, with Tyler. He kissed me again, the same way, but for longer. Then he told me I was going to start helping him more. When he pulled into the parking lot, I could see that car from the other night and the same guy leaning against it. For some reason my heart started beating faster, but then Tyler leaned over and gently pulled my chin toward him. You're so hot. You know that, don't you? All the fear in me disappeared.

It was no big deal. All I had to do was give the guy some money and he gave me a small bag to give to Tyler. It was as easy as delivering a pizza. He even gave me a tip, twenty bucks. He said not to tell Tyler. It could be our secret. I didn't like the way he smiled at me when he said that. He even touched my neck. If Tyler saw that he wouldn't like it. I slipped the money in my jeans and said thanks.

Tyler kissed me again and told me I was a natural. I liked that, because it means I'm good at something not everyone can learn. We delivered pizzas until almost midnight. When Tyler dropped me off he said he was really glad that I had made a good impression on his friend. He reminded me that who you know is more important than what you know and I know that must be true. Look at my mom. She doesn't know anyone important and that's why she's doing what she's doing. And that's why, thanks to Tyler, I'm going to be doing something very different when I'm her age.

CHAPTER TWENTY-ONE

TESSA

The picture Alex gave us is now hanging on the fridge. I look at it first thing before leaving and I think about him and the story he told us all day, even as I think ahead to what I'm planning to do after school.

After the last bell rings and the halls empty out, I roll up the long piece of paper that was hanging on Krista's locker, to make it look like a scroll, and tie it with the yellow ribbon I brought from home. It's the one we used to tie around the railing of our tiny balcony when my dad came home on leave. My mom wasn't into all that "army hocus-pocus," but she didn't want him to feel left out. What if all his fellow soldiers had yellow ribbons wrapped around banisters and trees and he ended up feeling unloved?

Paul is walking Annie home for me so I can go straight to Krista's. The three of us walk as far together as we can. Paul says good luck and then he does something totally unexpected. He kisses my cheek real fast. I can feel myself blush under my scarf. I hope Annie won't blab to our mother. She has told me a million times to leave boys alone until I finish school and get that scholarship. She says it like she knows the money is just sitting there waiting for me and all I have to do is grab it.

I feel like I'm delivering a diploma when Krista's mom lets me in.

"Tessa," she says, giving me a hug at the front door. "Thank you so much for coming. Not just today, but all the other times too. I don't know what to do. I just don't. I haven't been able to get a word out of Krista today."

She looks so official in her nurse's uniform, like she should have all the answers. If she doesn't, how can I? I hide the scroll from her. I want Krista to see it first.

"She's in her room. You go on in and try to cheer her up. I have to go but I hate leaving her like this. Her dad has to work late, so I'm so glad you're here." She calls out goodbye to Krista, throws on her coat, and leaves.

Krista is rolled in a ball, as usual. Her blanket is shaking, like she's crying. I lean over her, the scroll in my hand, ready to be unfurled. It will be like a proclamation from the olden days, with the paper trailing on the ground and someone important reading the news in a deep and booming voice. I'll read the comments to her and she'll brighten up. Some of them are really lovely, better than I imagined. Even Ms. Bane stopped by to write that she was sorry she hadn't called but that she was thinking about Krista and hoped she'd come back soon.

Except, when I bend closer, I see that she isn't crying. She's shivering and sweat is rolling off her forehead. I shake her shoulder to see if I can get her attention. When she opens her eyes, all I see are the whites. I scream and drop the scroll. I run down the hall, hoping her mom is still putting on her shoes in the porch, but she isn't and there is no sign of her outside. Didn't she see the state Krista is in? Maybe she hadn't gone up close enough to see that Krista was shaking. Or she saw it and thought she was just crying, like I had.

Krista's dad is working late. I am completely alone. I run back to Krista, hoping I'll find her better, but she's the same, maybe worse. I call her name but she doesn't answer. I don't think she even heard me.

I grab the phone beside her bed and dial 9-1-1. Krista might be angry, but it's no longer up to her. Krista was always sending me away. She told me she had never felt better, now that she was losing weight, and that I couldn't understand. And then I think about those pills, sandwiched in her bed. I reach down and pull out the bottle. It's almost empty. The label says *90 tablets. Take one per day.* But that can't be right. Krista has been home for about three weeks. I remember the Websites I Googled and all that they said about diet pills and their dangers. They even mentioned heart attacks.

I scribble a note for Krista's dad and by the time the paramedics arrive, twenty minutes later, I'm ready. I'm amazed by how level-headed I feel. Then, in the ambulance, with Krista still trembling on a gurney beside me, I almost lose it. I grab her hand and hold it the whole way, squeezing hard. I have a feeling I'm her anchor. If I let go she'll float away, like an astronaut in the space station, turning and tumbling without gravity.

At the hospital, the paramedics wheel Krista into the Emergency area and transfer her onto a narrow bed pushed against the wall. I stand beside her as doctors and nurses bustle around us. Finally, a young doctor in a blue coat takes Krista's pulse and flashes a light into her pupils. Then he turns to me.

"What's the story here? What happened?"

"She was shaking and I couldn't get her to talk to me."

"But where was she? What was she doing? Were you at school?"

"No, she was at home, in bed."

"Why? Was she having health problems? Was she sick?"

"She was having emotional problems. She didn't want to eat."

"Do you know if she's diabetic?"

"I don't think so."

"Any other medical conditions?"

"No, but . . ."

My heart beats loudly and I suck in my breath.

"Please go on. If there's anything you need to tell me . . ."

Krista wouldn't want him knowing about her pills. He'll have to tell her parents and she won't be happy about that. But what if what I know could save her? What if, years from now when I do become a doctor, I look back on this moment and realize that I hadn't shared the one piece of information that could have saved Krista's life? That I had kept silent and let her lie out there on a burning field without trying to pull her to safety.

I let out my breath with a whoosh. "Actually, she's taking diet pills. She's been taking them for weeks, since she stopped going to school."

"Okay, good to know. Do you know what kind?"

"Yes, I have them." I pull out the bottle and hand it over. The doctor frowns as he reads the label. "I wasn't supposed to know, but I saw them in her room. I think she got them off the Internet." He shakes his head.

"That was smart, bringing these here. Good thinking."

He smiles down at me and for the first time I really believe that I might be able to do what he does one day. "Okay, in there." He points out a room to two orderlies and they wheel Krista inside. "She'll be fine. Have a seat."

But I don't sit. Instead, I take the elevator up to the Neonatal Unit. This might be another thing Krista will hate me for, but I have to get her mom. If it were me or Annie down in Emergency my mom would want to be there, not just floors above us, totally in the dark.

Krista's mom is placing a baby into a bassinette when I find her. I wait until the baby is settled before tapping on the glass. Her face turns white when she sees me. She rushes out and I tell her everything, except about the pills. I betrayed Krista to the doctor but it will be up to her to tell her parents. And I can't help feeling that if her parents hadn't been so blind, they would've found the pills in the first place. It didn't take a genius to see that Krista was in seriously bad shape.

An hour later, Krista is in a hospital bed with an IV drip in her arm. Her mom and dad are in the room, one on either side of her. Krista's eyes are open and she looks calm.

"Oh, honey. You scared us," Krista's dad says.

"You sure did, Krista," adds her mom. "I can't believe this happened. That I didn't know."

Krista's dad puts his arm around his wife. "Never mind. She's okay now, thanks to Tessa." Krista's parents look over at me and smile.

"I'm glad you're alright, Krista," I say. "I have to go now. My mom will be worried." I know they have a lot to talk about and I don't need to be there when they do. Krista nods but doesn't speak.

"I'll drive you home," Krista's dad says.

"No, it's okay. I can take the bus. Please, don't leave Krista. I'll be fine. I know my way." My mom's café is a block away, so I really do.

Walking from the bus to home in the dark, past the pizzeria, my heart quickens. I'm on the other side of the street this time, but still, I don't know what I'd do if I saw Chelsea. Only she isn't there. She's out somewhere, getting messed up in her boyfriend's deals and pushed around. I wonder who else knows. Is there anyone who can tell Chelsea's mom what's happening to her? Would her mom care? I have no idea and, I decide as I turn into our courtyard, I can't spend too much time thinking about it. I can't save everyone. Maybe when I'm a doctor I'll try. But right now, I have enough people on my plate.

My mom knows where I've been because Krista's mom called her. She's full of questions. I tell her everything, even about the pills. She'll know that I've known about them all along and possibly be disappointed in me. But I did what I thought a good friend should do. I put Krista first, both by not telling and then, today, by telling. Maybe my mom gets that too.

CHELSEA

Tyler took me to an expensive store to buy me a party dress, one I could never afford myself. It has thin straps and no back and it's super short. It's for a party Tyler is taking me to at his friend's place tomorrow, the one who gave me twenty bucks, the one who might be able to get me into modelling. I watched a show about three young models who were doing a round of big parties in Manhattan. They were stepping out of a white limo, their long legs all tangled. A few hours later, they stumbled back into it, tugging at their short skirts. Their mouths were always open, laughing, and their clothes were so shiny. Inside the clubs, silver buckets of ice and champagne sat at every table. I keep wondering if the party Tyler is taking me to will be like that.

Tyler said no one there will know how young I am. Then he said guys will like that I'm so young. "The younger the better," he said. He said I can just be myself, no matter what happens. No matter what anyone asks me to do, just be myself. I'll tell my mom I'm going to a dance at school. That will make her happy. She'll think I'm developing school spirit or something.

I'll start getting ready early, in the middle of the day. I'll keep my door closed. I'll be able to hear my mother vacuuming and washing the kitchen and bathroom, like she does every Saturday. I'll listen to those noises as I put my make-up on and squeeze into my new dress. And I'll feel so good that I am getting out of here, one big step at a time.

CHAPTER TWENTY-TWO

I go to the hospital after dinner today. "Straight there and back," my mom says as I'm leaving. "And call before you leave so I can meet you at the corner." She doesn't like the way I walked it alone last time. I start to protest, but stop. At least she's letting me go.

I'm glad I have the bus ride to think about what I'm going to say. I could say sorry but I'm not sorry. I'm glad I told about the pills. I only hope Krista understands why I did it.

Krista's dad is in the room when I get there. He's sitting on the chair, bent over, his hands clasped, almost like he's praying. He's way too big for the chair and he seems to be fighting the urge to spring out of it. He isn't saying anything but I can hear lots of words going round in his head.

"Tessa. How nice. Look, Krista, Tessa came to see you." He stands, looking relieved for the distraction. "I'll go get a coffee, leave you two alone."

"Thanks," I say, approaching Krista slowly. Her eyes are open but she still hasn't looked at me.

"Hi, Krista. How are you doing?"

Krista shrugs. "Okay, I guess."

"You sure look better than yesterday." It's true. Colour has returned to her face and she's washed her hair.

"For now, maybe. But they'll force me to eat in here."

"I'm sorry, Krista. I had no choice. You were so sick. I had to tell."

"How did you know?"

"I saw the pills in your bed. I looked them up. They're pretty scary, you know?"

"Yeah, and so is eating and getting fatter."

"But you can't live the rest of your life without eating. You know that."

"I can't live the rest of my life eating, either. You don't know what it's like to be so big."

"Yeah, you're right. I don't." I wait a bit and then pull out the scroll. "I have something for you."

"What is it?" Krista's eyes lock on mine for the first time.

"Open it and see." Just then Krista's mother pops into the room. "Or do it later, when you're alone," I whisper, shoving the scroll under her blanket. Krista is good at hiding things in her bed and this time I'm glad. It's a private thing. She'll want to read the notes herself.

"Tessa. I thought I heard voices," her mom says.

"Hi, Mrs. Della Corte. I can't stay long. I told my mom I'd only stay a few minutes. I'll come back tomorrow, okay?" Krista's hand is still under the blanket, clutching the scroll. She nods and something like the tiniest smile curls her lips.

"I wanted to thank you, Tessa. For everything." Krista's mom looks down at her feet, like part of her is too embarrassed to look me in the eye. It must be even worse for her, because of what she does.

"You're welcome." I say it in a friendly way, to put her out of her misery. I mean, look at me and my mom with Annie. We never noticed those horrible drawings or Annie's confusion behind them. Maybe it's hard to see things in people when they're too close.

On the bus, I picture Krista reading the messages. I hope each one will sink in and make her see that most people do care. Sure, there are some nasty ones, but Paul and I decided not to rub them out. It's not like they'll shock Krista. The kind ones will surprise her more because nice kids don't form gangs and go around forcing their good deeds on people. There's no such thing as being assaulted by kindness or surrounded by circles of people wanting to praise you. Those things seem to happen quietly and where no one can see them. It's the bad stuff that always sticks out.

When Krista opens the scroll, she'll see the kindness in black and white, staring her right in the face, maybe for the first time.

CHELSEA

Earlier tonight, I covered up my dress with my coat in case my mom saw me leaving. I wore jeans underneath, too, planning to pull them off in the car on the way to the party. Tyler was picking me up at my door so I didn't have to walk anywhere and get splashed or sweaty. He said he wanted me in mint condition for the party, like a new coin that hadn't been circulated yet.

I called goodbye to my mom from the front door. She was in the bathroom with the water running, so I couldn't tell if she heard me or not. For some reason I wanted to open the door and say goodbye to her face, but I didn't. I'd never done that before and I couldn't start now. So I just called out goodbye again. I waited at the door to see if she'd come out, but she didn't.

The dress is hidden in the back of my closet now, along with the cashmere sweater. It smells like smoke and sweat and booze, all the smells of the party. We'd only been there twenty minutes when someone bumped into me and knocked my glass, spilling my drink. Tyler grabbed some napkins and helped me rub it off, but then I had a wet spot. Tyler didn't look too happy, but he still put his arm around my waist and took me around the smoky room, introducing me to his friends. They all seemed older than him and so did the other girls who were there. I felt so young, I might as well have been wearing knee socks. So I did what they did. I laughed when they laughed and I sipped from my tall glass when they did. Tyler got me another drink. It was fruity. It made my head fuzzy.

My mom can't ever find the dress. If she does, she'll want an explanation. I'd either have to lie or tell her about Tyler. And I can't tell anyone about him. Not now. Not after what happened at the party.

CHAPTER TWENTY-THREE

Today is one of those super bright fall days, where you can still feel the heat of summer in the air, but every now and then a gust of cold winter wind hits you. I grab this huge pair of sunglasses I bought in the summer and never wear. I can't decide if they suit me or not because they look like the kind of sunglasses Paris Hilton would wear. I pop them on and look in the mirror. I'm still just me with frizzy brown hair living my ordinary life with my ordinary family. And that's okay.

A while later, though, I feel extraordinary. That's because Paul and I are walking to the hospital from the bus stop, holding hands. We kick up piles of leaves as we walk through city squares, scaring the frenetic squirrels, and by the time we get there, our jeans are covered in colourful bits of foliage. We stop to shake them clean before going inside.

Krista is okay with meeting Paul. She thanks him for his comment and tells him she knew who he was when she read it. It turns out they were in Media class together. We don't stay that long. Krista's parents are coming by later to take her home, now that she's been rehydrated.

"Hey, who do you think you are? Paris Hilton?" Krista says when I put my sunglasses back on before leaving. I don't take it as an insult. I'm just glad to hear her laughing.

"If she was Paris Hilton, I wouldn't want to hang out with her," Paul says, surprising us both.

I never thought I'd hear a guy say that.

Later, I'm just getting into bed when my mom pops into my room to tell me that we received a package from Uncle Johnny. "There was a postcard for you in it," she says, handing it over.

I snuggle under my covers to read it. On the front is a picture of a man in a small boat, holding up a giant greenish fish with a big bubble head. I flip the card over and see it's from Malaysia. The fish is a dolphin-fish, or mahi mahi. It says, *Hey Tessa, I caught the best catch of my life today off the coast of the northern peninsula. It looks just like this one. I didn't think I could do it, but I did. My grin is ear to ear. This fish means I'm ready to go home. It tells me it's time, Tessa. With lots of love and affection, Uncle Johnny.*

What is he trying to tell me — that I should go out and fish? I think about it as I lie there: the fish, his challenge, having to push himself to do something he thought he couldn't do. Is that what I've done these last few weeks? Is that what Johnny is telling me? If so, what's my mahi mahi — everything I've done for Krista? Or is Johnny telling me that my biggest challenge is still to come and he wants me to know I can handle it?

One thing I know for sure is that there is always a new challenge around the corner. Sometimes it shocks you, like with Chelsea. Sometimes it kills you, like with my dad. Sometimes it helps you, like with Alex and what he told us.

Sometimes that thing makes you stronger, like I'm hoping the words on the scroll have done for Krista.

I tack Uncle Johnny's postcard on the wall above my bed so that I can fall asleep under the image of him holding the huge fish in his arms, his long legs straddling the boat, making it rock. Knowing Johnny, he slipped it back in the water. This was sport-fishing, not food-fishing. He once explained the difference. Catching the fish was a sign, a symbol. That's all he needed. I hope he'll get a warm welcome when he gets home. There won't be any yellow ribbons but I hope my Aunt Stacey will open her arms and take him in.

I know that's what I'd do.

I'm just about to fall asleep when I remember that my mom mentioned a package. What else did Johnny send? I find her in the living room, sipping a glass of wine, her feet up on the coffee table.

"Hey, Mom," I say. "What is all that?" A pile of papers sits on the couch beside her.

"Your Uncle Johnny is quite a man, you know. I never really knew him well when your dad was here because they didn't get along. I'm not sure why — they seem so alike to me. Anyhow, Johnny sent some pictures of him and your dad as kids, from their mom's stuff. But he also sent this." She hands me two slips of paper.

"Oh my god," I say. In my hand is a cheque for fifty thousand dollars, along with a note. *Dear Sam, Mom never said to split the money, so I didn't. I thought because I'd stayed to look after her and clean up all her financial mess, I didn't have to. But I was wrong. It just took me a decade to realize it. Lots of love, Johnny.*

"I never thought I'd see a cheque like that from your

dad's family, not in this lifetime," says my mom.

We just sit there, side by side. I listen to her sip her wine and sigh. I guess she's thinking the same as me: What will we do with the money?

"Will we move, Mom?"

"We'll see, Tessa. We'll see. It's a lot of money but it's not enough for a house. A down payment for sure, but then there are lots of expenses after that. We'll see. It'll take the edge off, at least, and it'll go a long way toward college for you and Annie, along with the other money." She doesn't say the money for my dad's death but I know what she means.

"For now, let's say we get you a new fall jacket—that old one is looking very tattered— and a computer. How does that sound?"

"It sounds perfect, Mom." And it does. In fact, I can't think of anything else I need.

Today, my dad kissed my forehead and called me his princess. For a second, I stiffened. I thought he was going to start lying again about how beautiful I am. But when he picked up a piece of my hair and twirled it around his finger, I let go. He didn't seem to be pretending, especially when his eyes filled with tears. Maybe I really am his princess.

My mom was in the kitchen, cooking. She made a deal with me: I don't have to go back to school as long as I attend Dr. Hatrioff's session once a week. I can do my school work at home. She arranged it with Mr. Steinbrenner. Ms. Bane has already sent a bundle of stuff, including the flyer for this year's writing contest.

The scroll that Tessa gave me is hanging above my bed. I reread it a lot. Why didn't Kate ever ask me to join the volleyball team? And who's April, the girl who knows that beauty is only skin deep? Is she heavy like me? And what about Sam, who wants girls for real beauty to unite? Even the fact that Chelsea wrote something amazes me, even if it was mean. What surprised me was how I really don't care. Jamal is right, Chelsea is a bitch. She doesn't mean anything to me. Neither does Amber, who says the caf is "loosing" money without me. Jennifer, the cheerleader, has a good point—Chelsea and Amber don't own the school. And, like Tessa said, I can't let them win.

CHELSEA

Tyler texted me and told me to wear the cashmere sweater and short skirt tonight. When I pulled the sweater out of my hiding place in the closet it smelled like the party because of the dress. It was days ago but the smell is still strong. It nearly choked me as I pulled the sweater on.

I haven't seen Tyler since the party. I don't understand why he left me alone with that guy. All of a sudden Tyler was gone and *he* was there, putting his arm around me and reminding me about the twenty-buck tip he'd given me. "Payback time," he said, and I was confused, because usually you don't have to pay tips back. And Tyler just watched us walk off. I know because I turned to look for him, knowing he wouldn't let anything bad happen to me. He'd take one look and come over to get me, maybe even punch the guy for what he was trying. But when I found him he was watching us and smiling.

The TV hums through the wall and I wonder what my mom is watching. If she knew I was going out, would she stop me? Would she even want me to stay in and watch TV with her? As I sit here on my bed writing, the cashmere feels tight, so tight it's like it's gripping me, making it hard to breathe. If I cough really loud, maybe my mother will hear me.

ACKNOWLEDGEMENTS

Thank you to Jane, who listened to an early draft by the ocean and gave great advice; to my clever daughter, Cassandra, who convinced me to downplay a certain celebrity who already gets way too much attention; to Ron, whose unconditional and constant support keeps me writing; and to Louise, who helped me figure it out and made me laugh. Thanks also to all the awesome people in my family, who all love to read and make books a big part of their lives. This book was written with the support of the Conseil des arts et des lettres du Québec, so thank you to them as well.

ABOUT THE AUTHOR

LORI WEBER grew up in Park Extension, a vibrant neighbourhood in Montreal. She taught English in Nova Scotia and
Newfoundland before returning to Quebec. She now splits
her time between teaching English at John Abbott College and
writing books for young people in her home in Pointe-Claire,
where she lives with her husband and two cats. She has published seven young adult novels and has ideas for many more.
Find out more about Lori at www.lori-weber.com.